P9-BZO-371
BOOTH
Written by C.C. Colbert
Illustrated by Tanitoc
Color by Hilary Sycamore
:01
First Second

:01
First Second
New York & London

Published by First Second
First Second is an imprint of Roaring Brook Press,
a division of Holtzbrinck Publishing Holdings Limited Partnership,
175 Fifth Avenue, New York, NY 10010

Distributed in Canada by H. B. Fenn and Company Ltd.
distributed in the United Kingdom by Macmillan Children's Books,
a division of Pan Macmillan.

Design by Colleen AF Venable

Colored by Hilary Sycamore and Blue Sky Ink. Lead Colorist: Sarah Karloff

Cataloging-in-Publication Data is on file at the Library of Congress.

ISBN: 978-1-59643-125-6

First Second books are available for special promotions and premiums.
For details, contact: Director of Special Markets, Holtzbrinck Publishers.

First Edition April 2010
Printed in China
1 3 5 7 9 10 8 6 4 2

Chapter 1

Wherein:

- We meet the subject of our tale, John Wilkes Booth, and become acquainted with his family, opinions, and temperament.

- A gathering of their theatrical family leads to a falling out between Booth and his brother, Edwin.

- Booth departs for unknown business. A loyal supporter of thc confederacy, he has already embarked on a life of subterfuge....

V.
N. E.
N.Y.
R.
N. C.
S. C
N. J.

HENRY IV, WILLIAM SHAKESPEARE

NOT WORTH A GOOSEBERRY.
YOU, THAT ARE OLD,
CONSIDER NOT THE CAPACITIES OF US THAT ARE YOUNG:
YOU MEASURE THE HEAT OF OUR LIVERS
WITH THE BITTERNESS
OF YOUR GALLS:
AND WE THAT ARE IN THE WAYWARD OF OUR YOUTH,
I MUST CONFESS,
ARE WAGS TOO."
BRAVO! BRAVO!
Mr. BOOTH, YOUR SONS WILL SURELY FOLLOW YOUR PATH!
CLAP! CLAP!
SPEAKING OF WHICH: WHERE'S YOUR BROTHER ?
JOHN? I'M SURE HE'S NEAR BY, FATHER.

1863
V.
N.E.
N.C.
N.Y.
R.
S.C
N.J.
JOIN, or DIE.
AFTER TWO YEARS OF A WAR THAT HAS RIPPED APART THE UNITED STATES, NO ONE ON EITHER SIDE IS SO ARROGANT ANY MORE AS TO THINK THE VICTORY INEVITABLE.
THE TIMES PIT BROTHER AGAINST BROTHER,
EDWIN BOOTH
HAMLET
STAR-THEAT
AND NO FAMILY IS MORE DIVIDED THAN THE FAMED THEATRICAL DYNASTY, THE BOOTHS...
EDWIN, CLEAR HEIR TO HIS FATHER'S THESPIAN THRONE, SIDES WITH THE UNION.
HIS YOUNGER BROTHER, JOHN, A SELF-STYLED SOUTHERN GENTLEMAN ...
STAFF ONLY
...AND A CONFEDERATE FROM THE FIRST SALVO...

...IS INCREASINGLY DRAWN INTO THE WEB OF UNSANCTIONED ESPIONAGE.
JOHN WILKES BOOOTH: A TRIUMPH AS ROMEOOO!
VOLUNTEER WANTED
$ TOTAL TO NEW RECRUI
TRIUMPH
NEW YORK TIMES
office
COME, PEACE! NOT LIKE A MOURNER BOWED ‹‹ FOR HONOR LOST AN' DEAR ONES WASTED, ‹‹ BUT PROUD, TO MEET A PEOPLE PROUD, WITH EYES THET TELL OF TRIUMPH TASTED! ›
WIDE
AWAKE

AT THE BOOTH HOME, TUDOR HALL – CHRISTMAS 1863
I MUST GO OUT TO CHECK ON THE MEAL, BUT YOU WILL LET ME KNOW AS SOON AS JOHNNIE GETS HERE...
YES, OF COURSE. I'VE ALREADY...
YOU PROMISE TO LET ME KNOW THE MOMENT HE COMES...
I PROMISE!
I PROMISE!
WELL, EDWIN, THE WAR DOESN'T SEEM TO HAVE SLAKED THE PUBLIC THIRST FOR DRAMA.
I HEAR YOUR HAMLET IS BOOKED SOLID.
WE'RE SO PROUD OF EDWIN. HIS FATHER WOULD BE SO PROUD.
YES, I'M SURE HE'D GIVE THE SLAVES AN EXTRA RATION OF CORNPONE TO EXPRESS HIS JOY.
EDWIN!
JOHNNIE SEEMS TO BE GETTING GOOD REVIEWS...

THEN IMAGINE HOW GOOD THEY'D BE IF HE REMEMBERED HE'S AN ACTOR AND NOT A POLITICIAN.
EDWIN, YOU PROMISED ...
IT'S NO SECRET TO OUR COUSINS THAT CONFLICTING LOYALTIES DIVIDE OUR FAMILY— JUST AS THEY DO THE NATION.
LET'S TRY
TO KEEP OUR PROMISES FOR A PLEASANT HOLIDAY.
LET'S AT LEAST HAVE ANOTHER TOAST:
MAY THIS WAR BE OVER BEFORE WE SEE ANOTHER CHRISTMAS!
HEAR! HEAR!
MERRY CHRISTMAS
1863
TO PEACE!

TO THE UNION RESTORED!

WHAT'S GOTTEN INTO YOU?
JOHNNIE'S NOT EVEN HERE YET AND YOU'RE SPOILING FOR A FIGHT!
DO YOU EXPECT ME...
...TO TOAST THE CONFEDERACY?
IF YOU PROVOKE YOUR BROTHER...
I WON'T RUFFLE HIS BANTAM FEATHERS
FOR MY SAKE...

WELCOME HOME, JOHNNIE!
MERRY CHRISTMAS!
WHERE IS MY FAVORITE NIECE?

HERE, UNCLE JOHN!
"UNCLE JOHN," MUSIC TO MY EARS.
LOOK WHAT I BROUGHT!
!?
WHAT IS ALL THIS?
A CHRISTMAS TREE...
I BOUGHT IT IN GERMANTOWN: YOU DECORATE IT FOR THE HOLIDAYS.
MAMA, LOOK AT THIS!
WHERE IS HE?
MERRY
JOHN, IT'S GOOD TO SEE YOU...
THE PRODIGAL RETURNS!
FAR FROM PRODIGAL, EDWIN.

I WAS THE ONE AT HOME WHEN FATHER DIED...
AND I INVEST MY MONEY AS WISELY AS MY TIME...
... DESPITE WHAT SOME MIGHT THINK.
TODAY, I HAVE NO QUARREL WITH YOU, BROTHER.
LET THERE BE PEACE ON EARTH AND GOOD WILL TOWARD BOOTHS
— AT LEAST FOR TODAY!
WHAT'S KEEPING YOU UP, BROTHER?
THE MEMORIES OF THIS PLACE.
JOIN ME?
I CAN'T. THERE'S SOMETHING I NEED TO TAKE CARE OF. I'LL ONLY BE GONE A FEW HOURS ...
SO IF YOU CAN LET MOTHER KNOW...

FOR GOD'S SAKE, JOHN, IT'S CHRISTMAS DAY!
THIS CONCERNS IMPORTANT BUSINESS.
WHAT KIND OF BUSINESS ?
I'M NOT AT LIBERTY TO DISCUSS...
LISTEN, LITTLE BROTHER...
...WHAT YOU DO WITH YOUR LIFE IS NONE OF MY CONCERN...
LET'S KEEP IT THAT WAY.
... BUT AS A HEAD OF THIS FAMILY ...
YOU'RE **NOT** MY FATHER !!
NO, BUT IF HE WERE HERE, HE'D TELL YOU TO KEEP OUT OF THE SPYGAME.
I'M NOT A SPY.
WHATEVER IT IS YOU DO BEHIND CONFEDERATES LINES...

DON'T YOU THINK EVERYONE KNOWS?
ARE YOU WILLING TO RISK YOUR FAMILY...
YOU'VE GOT A LOT OF NERVE LECTURING ME ABOUT FAMILY!
MARY'S WORRIED SICK ABOUT YOUR DRINKING AND YOU'RE ON THE ROAD ALL THE TIME.
I DOUBLE MY INCOME ON TOUR!
HAVE YOU TURNED INTO A PROPER YANKEE? MONEY GRUB-BING WHILE YOUR FAMILY LANGUISHES ?!
WERE YOU THINKING OF FAMILY WHEN YOUR LEADING LADY STABBED YOU IN THE FACE?
THAT WAS A PRIVATE MISUNDER-STANDING!
NOT WHEN YOU DRAG MY NAME INTO THE HEADLINE!
"HE THAT FILCHES FROM ME MY GOOD NAME ROBS ME OF THAT WHICH ENRICHES HIM AND MAKES ME POOR INDEED."
NO NEED TO QUOTE SHAKESPEARE TO ME, BROTHER...

...WE HAD THE SAME TEACHER.
KEEP YOUR VOICES DOWN —YOU'LL WAKE THE WHOLE HOUSE!
WHAT IS GOING ON?
EDWINA IS BOUND TO COME DOWNSTAIRS ANY MINUTE.
NOTHING.
I'M LEAVING.
PLEASE DON'T;
EDWINA WILL BE SO DISAPPOINTED!
JOHNNIE, WHATEVER EDWIN HAS BEEN SAYING...
I'LL BE BACK IN TWO SHAKES OF A LAMB'S TAIL,
WITH ANOTHER SADDLEBAG FULL OF PRESENTS.

Chapter 2

Wherein:

- We are introduced to John Wilkes Booth's co-conspirators: a ragtag gang of confederate sympathizers who congregate in the Round House pub.
- Booth is recruited into a deeper game of espionage.
- At a benefit for the war wounded, Booth loses his heart to a woman whose political leanings mirror his brother Edwin's: pro-union.

DURING THE SUMMER OF 1864, WASHINGTON BECOMES THE CENTER OF INTRIGUE.
BEER
SOUTHERN SYMPATHIZERS AND CONFEDERATE SECRET AGENTS ROAM THE CITY.
...AND WHEN I HEARD THE NEWS,
I JUST LEAPT FROM THE STAGE AND BORROWED A GUN,
AND HEADED OFF TO FIND OLD JOHN BROWN.
WHAT WILL YOU HAVE?
YOU WERE WITH THE RICHMOND GRAYS?
THE DAY WE CAPTURED BROWN AND THE DAY HE WAS HANGED.
YOU'RE NOT SQUEAMISH WHEN IT COMES TO A HANGING, Mr. BOOTH.

DEPENDS ...
ON WHO'S DOING THE HANGING ...
AND WHO'S AT THE END OF THE ROPE.
IF YOU'RE AS MUCH A SON OF THE SOUTH AS YOU SAY YOU ARE, YOU MIGHT TAKE A RIDE OUT TO ARLINGTON PIKE ...
... NEAR PEARSON'S. ABOUT FOUR O'CLOCK TOMORROW.
WHY SHOULD I ?
"WITH CAIN GO WANDER THROUGH SHADES OF NIGHT ..."
"... AND NEVER SHOW THY HEAD BY DAY NOR LIGHT."
FOUR O'CLOCK
AND COME ALONE.

THE NEXT DAY
HERE IS A QUIET PLACE TO TALK.
...AND I WON'T SIT BY AND WATCH THE COLLAPSE OF ALL OUR HOPES! ...
HERE HE COMES ...
LOOK!
?!

!

AS BOOTH OBSERVES LINCOLN, HE HIMSELF IS OBSERVED

BOOTH DEPARTS...
...AND HIS RECRUITERS COMPARE NOTES.
HOW'D IT GO?
HE'S A TRUE BELIEVER.
AND LINCOLN?
BROUGHT HIM UP EVEN BEFORE HE CAME RIDING BY... SAYS HE HATES HIM...
HE COULD BE JUST WHAT WE'RE LOOKING FOR...
BUT AN ACTOR...
WE NEED NEW BLOOD!
BUT OUR ORDERS FROM RICHMOND...
RICHMOND!
RICHMOND IS ALL TALK! WE NEED ACTION.
WE'LL WORK OUR OPERATIONS OUT OF CANADA FROM NOW ON.
KEEP A CLOSE WATCH ON HIM.
WHATEVER YOU SAY, BOSS!

LATER
THAT NIGHT
SANITARY COMMISSION
CHARITY BALL

CHARITY BALL

NOW THAT YOU HAVE OUTSHONE ALL THE OTHER WOMEN ON THE DANCE FLOOR ...

... YOU COME OUTSIDE TO SHAME THE MOON, MISS?
I CAME OUTSIDE TO BE BY MYSELF, Mr. BOOTH.
AH! YOU'RE A THEATERGOER.
PERHAPS YOU'VE SEEN ME ON STAGE?
MORE LIKELY FERGUSON'S OR THE STAR SALOON.
...
IF...
...MY COMPANY IS ...SO UNWELCOME...
ANY NUMBER OF WOMEN INSIDE WOULD GIVE THEIR EYETEETH FOR YOUR COMPANY.
BUT NOT YOU.

NO.
I'M QUITE ATTACHED TO MY EYE-TEETH.
ARE YOU ATTACHED
IN ANY OTHER WAY?
ONLY TO MY FREEDOM.
SHE'S A BEAUTY, THAT'S FOR SURE!
SHE'S OFTEN AT THE WHITE HOUSE WHEN LINCOLN'S OLDER SON IS HOME.
WHO IS SHE?
SENATOR HALE'S DAUGHTER.
THE ABOLITIONIST FROM NEW HAMPSHIRE!?

YES.
SHE'S BLUEBLOOD AND BLUESTOCKING.
SHE WON'T LET YOU "WHISTLE DIXIE," IF YOU GET MY DRIFT.
YOU WEREN'T PLANNING TO LEAVE WITHOUT SAYING GOOD-BYE...
...
WERE YOU, MISS HALE?
MY CARRIAGE IS HERE.
I'LL CALL ON YOU SOON.
CLAC!
IF I MAY.
PERHAPS.

AT THE SANITARY COMMISSION HEADQUARTERS
GOOD MORNING, LUCY!
I'M GLAD YOU COULD COME, EDWIN.
YOU'VE BEEN SUCH A GENEROUS DONOR!
ANYTHING I CAN DO ?
DON'T STAND ON CEREMONY ...
I'VE BEEN THINKING ABOUT A THEATRICAL BENEFIT...
...A CHARITY PERFORMANCE TO RAISE MONEY.
JUNIUS IS ON THE ROAD AND WON'T BE BACK UNTIL SOME TIME IN THE FALL,
AND JOHNNIE, WELL,
JOHNNIE ISN'T TOO RELIABLE ...
NOT RELIABLE?
HE WOULDN'T BE RECEPTIVE TO ANYTHING I SUGGEST ...
ESPECIALLY IF IT HELPS THE UNION.

WE'RE AT ODDS RIGHT NOW...
... HAVE BEEN FOR SOME TIME...
HOW LONG?
SANI
ALL DONAT WELC
JOHNNIE WAS STILL AT HOME WHEN OUR FATHER'S OTHER WIFE SHOWED UP FROM ENGLAND.
THE GOSSIP ...
HIS REMARRIAGE TO OUR MOTHER...
THE DIVORCE ...
JOHN WAS HOME FOR ALL OF IT.
I DIDN'T MEAN TO DREDGE UP PAINFUL MEMORIES ...
JOHNNIE WAS TOO YOUNG TO HANDLE THE SCANDAL.
HE WAS CALLED NAMES AT SCHOOL.
GO

Chapter 3

Wherein:

- A romance blooms! The attachment between Booth and Lucy Hale deepens, only to be complicated by the introduction of another suitor: Robert Todd Lincoln.

- At the Round House, Booth nurses his wounds and finds comfort with Ella, a woman of questionable virtue.

- Booth, now banned from the Hale mansion, continues his courtship of Lucy covertly, touching her heart with letters and gifts.

JOHN WILKES BOOTH CONTINUES HIS APPOINTED ROUNDS

MISS HALE, SENATOR!

SIR?
SIR, SENATOR HALE SAYS...
...COME INSIDE INSTEAD OF HIDING IN THE BUSHES...
I MIGHT HAVE CALLED A CONSTABLE.

YES, I SEE, WELL
ANY BROTHER OF EDWIN'S WEL-COME HERE.
MAKE YOURSELF AT HOME.
I'M SURE YOU KNOW EVERYBODY.
MY MOTHER DOESN'T WANT ME TO ENLIST,
BUT NOW THAT I'VE GRADUATED,...
SURELY YOUR FATHER CAN GET YOU A PLUM ASSIGNMENT!

WITH ALL THE BEST MEN OFF TO FIGHT, SOCIETY HAS LET DOWN THE BAR...
WOULDN'T YOU SAY?
SURELY SOME MEN NEED TO STAY BEHIND AND KEEP THINGS RUNNING...
DO YOU SUPPORT MILITARY EXEMPTION, Mr. BOOTH?
I THINK THE TWENTY NIGGER LAW MAKES SENSE.
I WAS TALKING ABOUT THE UNION ARMY, SIR!
BOTH ARMIES ALLOW THE POOR MAN TO TAKE A RICH MAN'S PLACE.

YANKEES NOW HAVE THEIR NIGGERS DOING THEIR FIGHTING.
SINCE THE EMANCIPATION PROCLAMATIO
SLAVERY MAY HAVE ENDED IN THE UNION, BUT THE CONFEDERACY IS KEEPING IT ALIVE...
AND WHAT KEEPS YOU FROM ENLISTING?
I HUMBLY FOLLOW IN THE FOOTSTEPS OF MY FATHER, JUNIUS BRUTUS BOOTH.
MY FATHER SAW YOU PERFORM IN "THE MARBLE HEART" LAST FALL, Mr. BOOTH, AND VERY MUCH ENJOYED YOUR PERFORMANCE!
PERHAPS I COULD ARRANGE FOR TICKETS FOR YOU AND YOUR FATHER.
HA! HA HA HA HA! HA
HA! HA! HA!
I'M SORRY, I DON'T GET THE JOKE!

HIS FATHER CAN GET HIS OWN TICKETS!
THIS IS ROBERT TODD LINCOLN.
YES,
PLEASED TO MEET YOU, Mr. BOOTH!
...
E... EXCUSE ME, I MUST BE GOING!
ALL THAT MALARKEY ABOUT HIS FATHER...
EVERYONE KNOWS...
THE BOOTHS ARE ALL BASTARDS!
WOULD YOU CARE TO REPEAT THAT, SIR?
THERE'S NO NEED ...
STEP OUTSIDE AND REPEAT YOURSELF!

IT IS YOU, Mr. BOOTH, WHO'D BEST BE STEPPING OUTSIDE.
CATO, PLEASE SHOW OUR GUEST THE WAY OUT!
I DON'T NEED A NIGGER TO SHOW ME THE DOOR!
LATER, AT THE ROUND HOUSE
I WISH I COULD HAVE SEEN YOU!
THAT PUP BETTER STAND GUARD OVER HIS DADDY IF HE WANTS TO KEEP SLEEPING IN THE WHITE HOUSE.
ROUND HOUSE
YOU'D NEVER TURN DOWN A CHANCE TO SLEEP IN THE WHITE HOUSE,
WOULD YOU, ELLA?
HA HA!
THERE'S NO NEED FOR THAT KIND OF TALK.
C'MON, NOW, CLYDE,
ELLA'S WORKING FOR THE CAUSE!
DEEPLY SORRY!

WORKING ON HER BACK MOST OF THE TIME!
TAKE THAT BACK!
OW!
S' TAK!
CLYDE DIDN'T MEAN ANY HARM.
ELLA KNOWS I WAS JUST JOSHING HER...
AW, BOSS!
ELLA GETS RESULTS,
WHICH IS MORE THAN I CAN SAY ABOUT YOU!
WHERE'S THAT QUININE YOU WERE SUPPOSED TO GET LAST WEEK?
I'M STILL WORKING ON IT!
THIS BLOCKADE IS KILLING OUR SOLDIERS BY THE THOUSANDS!
SO TIME'S A-WASTING ...
CLYDE, HOW ABOUT YOU HEADING OUT TO FORTRESS MONROE? THERE'S A SGT. FOSTER WITH A PALM ITCHING TO BE GREASED...
I WAS GOIN' ANYWAYS ...
WALK ME HOME ?

WHY WOULD Mr. BOOTH LEAVE WITHOUT SAYING GOOD-BYE?
PAPA, HE'S AN ACCOMPLISHED ACTOR!
HE WAS LUCKY TO ESCAPE WITHOUT A CANING.
DON'T GO TAKING IN ANOTHER STRAY, LUCY!
...
HE'S A HOTHEAD.
... TRIED TO CALL OUT ONE OF OUR GUESTS!
I'M SURE IT WAS A MISUNDERSTANDING! ...
DON'T GET DISTRACTED, ESPECIALLY WHEN WE'RE SO CLOSE TO OUR GOAL...
WE CAN'T RISK ANY SCANDAL!
YOU WILL GET AN AMBASSADORSHIP SOON – I'M SURE OF IT!
EXACTLY!
SO FORGET THIS WILKES FELLOW!
BUT, PAPA...
HE'S NO LONGER WELCOME IN THIS HOUSE, IS THAT UNDERSTOOD?
SUCH A GENTLEMAN, JOHNNIE!
MY JOHNNIE ...
AND YOU ARE THE LADY WHO KNOWS HOW TO PLEASE.
ELLA'S ROOM

I ALREADY TOLD YOU, JOHNNIE: I WON'T TAKE MONEY FROM YOU!
I THOUGHT WE HAD AN AGREEMENT!
WITHOUT ALL THE INFORMATION YOU GET ME, I WOULDN'T BE ABLE TO KEEP THIS OPERATION AFLOAT ...
I PAY YOU JUST LIKE I PAY THE OTHERS.
OOMS FOR ENT
WHEN WILL YOU TAKE ME TO CUBA, LIKE YOU PROMISED?
SOON LINCOLN WON'T BE RE-ELECTED AND THE NEW PRESIDENT IS SURE TO SIGN A TRUCE.
BUT, WHAT IF LINCOLN IS RE-ELECTED?
HE WON'T BE. BUT IF HE IS HE WON'T LIVE OUT HIS SECOND TERM ...
HOW CAN YOU BE SO SURE?
THE TRUE SONS OF THE SOUTH WILL MAKE SURE THE TYRANT IS DEPOSED. BUT FOR NOW, TAKE THE MONEY AND GET YOUR PICTURE MADE FOR ME.
AND HERE'S A LITTLE SOMETHING FOR YOU.

SECURITY IN WASHINGTON INCREASES AS THREATS TO THE PRESIDENT CONTINUE
I DON'T KNOW, CAPTAIN ...
HE KNEW THE SIGN AND ALL...
BUT HE WOULDN'T LOOK ME IN THE EYE.
JUST DIDN'T FEEL RIGHT.
YOUR HUNCH PAID OFF: MAPS AND TROOP STRENGTHS WERE HIDDEN IN HIS HATBAND.
PROBABLY DOESN'T CARE A WHISTLE 'BOUT THE REBS, BUT WILL SELL US OUT FOR THIRTY PIECES!
I'LL KEEP A CLOSE WATCH, SIR, YOU CAN COUNT ON ME!
I PLAN TO, Pvt. HARRIS!
REPORT IMMEDIATELY TO MY HEAD-QUARTERS!
THANK YOU, SIR!

ELSEWHERE
"AND NEVER SHOW THY HEAD BY DAY NOR LIGHT."
I COULDN'T GET ALL THE MAPS ...
...FELLOW GOT CAUGHT BY A PICKET.
WHAT ABOUT THE PLANS TO KIDNAP "STOVEPIPE"?
UNDER CONSIDERATION ...
YOU SAID THAT THE LAST TIME, BUT I HAVE FRIENDS ROTTING IN JAIL!
WE NEED TO GET PRISONER EXCHANGES GOING!
BE PATIENT AND, ABOVE ALL,
REMAIN ABOVE SUSPICION.
IT'S GONE BEYOND THAT BY NOW.
IF I GET CAUGHT EVERYONE I KNOW WILL BE IN THE DOCK WITH ME.
LET'S HOPE IT WON'T COME TO THAT.
TO VICTORY OR DEATH!

A LOVER'S GIFT
Booth
Wilki
J. W
My heart
stopped short
ny watch.
John

I'M SO GLAD YOU COULD COME!
IT SEEMED AS IF YOU WERE TALKING TO ME...
WILL YOU COME TO SUPPER?
NOT TONIGHT.
HOW MUCH LONGER DO WE HAVE TO SNEAK AROUND?
MY FATHER WILL BE APPOINTED SOON... IF WE CAN WAIT JUST A LITTLE LONGER...
TIME IS EXACTLY WHAT WE DON'T HAVE!
YOU KNOW HOW I FEEL ABOUT YOU!
THEN MEET ME ALONG ROCK CREEK, WHERE WE WERE RIDING YESTER-DAY!

I CAN MEET YOU BY FOUR.
HOW CAN I GET OUT OF HERE WITHOUT BEING SEEN?
I'LL SHOW YOU BACK STAIRS ONLY THE PLAYERS KNOW...
AND SO I OVERHEARD THE WOMAN SAY THAT HER HUSBAND WOULD LEAVE TOMORROW...
TO PROTECT A SHIPMENT OF GOLD...
GOOD WORK, DAVY! I KNEW THIS PHARMA-CY JOB WOULD PAY OFF.
WHAT SHOULD WE DO?
I NEED EACH OF YOU TO GO TO THESE LOCATIONS: THE NATIONAL HOTEL,
THE WILLARD,
AND TO FERGUSON'S
...AND ASK FOR ME.
MAKE SURE YOU START ASKING AROUND FOUR O'CLOCK.
WHERE ARE YOU GOING TO BE?
THAT DOESN'T MATTER...
IT JUST MATTERS THAT YOU ASK FOR ME.

ROCK CREEK
I'M GLAD YOU CAME...
I WAS AFRAID YOU MIGHT CHANGE YOUR MIND.
I WANT TO BE WITH YOU, JOHN!
AND YOU KNOW I WANT TO BE WITH YOU!
BUT ONLY IF YOU CAN BE SURE...
I'M HERE, AREN'T I?
UNDER OBSERVATION, AGAIN
I WISH I DIDN'T HAVE TO GO BACK!
OR WE COULD SHUT THE WHOLE WORLD OUT...
AND JUST GO ON BY OUR-SELVES...

BUT IF WE'RE GOING TO BE TOGETHER, YOU MUST BE HONEST WITH ME.
IS THIS FOR YOU OR FOR THE SENATOR?
LEAVE MY FATHER OUT OF THIS!
NOW... NOW THAT WE'RE... TOGETHER... WE HAVE TO BE ABLE TO TELL EACH OTHER EVERYTHING.
I'D LIKE TO, BUT YOUR FATHER KEEPS US APART!
THIS IS FOR ME, JOHN.
CAN YOU PROMISE NEVER TO BETRAY MY CONFIDENCE?
I PROMISE ...
YOU CANNOT BREATHE A WORD OF IT TO ANYONE —INCLUDING YOUR FATHER.
I LOVE YOU!
WELL, I LOVE MY HOME. I LOVE MARYLAND. I LOVE MY COUNTRY...
DON'T SPOUT PLATITUDES!
TELL ME THE TRUTH:

ARE YOU WORKING FOR THE ENEMY?
I'M NOT YOUR ENEMY, LUCY!
BUT IF YOU WORK TO DESTROY THE UNION, YOU'RE MY ENEMY!
I SMUGGLE QUININE AND OTHER MEDICAL SUPPLIES BEHIND ENEMY LINES.
THEN PAPA IS WRONG!!
SMUGGLING IS A HANGING OFFENSE...
RUNNING THE BLOCKADE...
WE ALL HATE THE BLOCKADE!
IT'S IMMORAL!
WHAT YOU'RE DOING IS HUMANITARIAN.
...AND TREASON!
NEVER! THAT'S WHY I DIDN'T WANT TO TELL YOU IN THE FIRST PLACE
BUT MAYBE I CAN HELP...
HAVE YOU TOLD EDWIN?
GOD, NO!!!
HE'D BE THE FIRST ONE TO TURN ME IN.
I THINK YOU'RE WRONG!
LUCY, YOU PROMISED NOT TO TELL A SOUL...
BUT I'M PROUD OF YOU!
NOW I UNDERSTAND!

Chapter 4

Wherein:

- Edwin Booth, in the height of his success, receives appalling news and quits the stage.
- Freed from the shadow of his brother's success, Booth rises in prominence in the theater—and in the world of conspiracy.
- When Lucy Hale convinces Edwin to return to the stage for a Booth family performance, she finds herself the target of her lover's jealousy and anger.

GROVER'S THEATER
WIN BOOTH
I PROMISED MARY I'D LOOK IN ON YOU, EDWIN.
I'M GLAD YOU DID!
EDWINA LOVED HER BIRTHDAY PRESENT...
MARY WONDERS WHEN YOU'LL GET CHILDREN OF YOUR OWN TO SPOIL.
HERALD
GROVER'S
AS A MATTER OF FACT, I'M THINKING ABOUT GETTING ENGAGED...
WHO IS IT THIS WEEK, JOHNNIE?
IT'S QUITE SERIOUS, I'VE BEEN COURTING LUCY HALE.

LUCY!
BUT HER FATHER'S A BLACK REPUBLICAN, WITH RUTHLESS AMBITION!!
WE'RE SEEING ONE ANOTHER IN SECRET. THE SENATOR DOESN'T THINK I'M GOOD ENOUGH TO WIPE LUCY'S SHOES!
MAYBE YOU THINK I'M RISING ABOVE MY STATION AS WELL...
I'VE NEVER IMPLIED ANYTHING OF THE SORT, IT'S JUST THAT—
KNOCK! KNOCK!
TEN MINUTES TO CURTAIN!
WE'LL CONTINUE THIS LATER.
I KNEW YOU WOULDN'T UNDERSTAND!
I HAVE TO GET READY TO GO ON!
YOU MUST OUTGROW THESE IMAGINED SLIGHTS!
SLAM!
EVERYTHING ALL RIGHT, GUV'NER?
DO NOT ADMIT MY BROTHER BACKSTAGE...
NOT EVER?
NOT BEFORE CURTAIN! NOT EVER AGAIN...

AT THE HEIGHT OF SUCCESS, TRAGEDY IS BREWING
TELEGRAM FOR EDWIN BOOTH !!
NO SPIT
NO SMOK
RICHAR
BRAVO!!
BRAV
VO!
HURR
A FEW WEEKS LATER
KNOCK! KNOCK!
Whiskey
FATHER AND I WANTED TO CONGRATULATE YOU.

I DIDN'T SEE YOU IN THE HOUSE TONIGHT...
ARE WE INTRUDING?
COME IN, COME IN!...
I HEARD MARY WAS ILL AND THOUGHT YOU MIGHT HAVE TO GO HOME.
I HAVE NO HOME.
WHAT?
Blank No. 1
THE WESTERN UNI
We regret to
you that your
beloved wife
died in her
sleep.
TELEGRAPH
HOW COULD I HAVE IGNORED THE WARNINGS?
YOU MUST GET BACK TO NEW YORK — TO MAKE ARRANGEMENTS.
THE RUN ISN'T HALF OVER.
FORGET THE SHOW. YOUR DAUGHTER...
YES OF COURSE, MY EDWINA!
WE'LL TAKE CARE OF THINGS HERE.
THAT MIGHT BE BEST FOR NOW.
I SWEAR, ON MY CHILD'S LIFE, I'LL NEVER TAKE ANOTHER DROP...
...AND NEVER SET FOOT ON STAGE AGAIN!
OH, EDWIN, YOU MUSTN'T SAY THAT!

I PROMISED MARY TO STAY HOME AND MANAGE A COMPANY
BUT NEVER GOT AROUND TO DOING IT.
YOU'LL STAY WITH US TONIGHT.
YOU DON'T HAVE TO BE ALONE.
YES, OF COURSE, EDWIN.
WHEN IS MOMMY COMING BACK ?
DON'T WORRY EDWINA, SHE'S IN A BEAUTIFUL PLACE FOR NOW.
EDWIN,
I'M SO SORRY.
I COULDN'T GET HERE SOONER, I WAS IN RICHMOND.
IT DOESN'T MATTER.
IF WE COULD JUST TURN BACK THE CLOCK,
IF I COULD GET BACK ALL THE TIME I WAS AWAY FROM HER!
TIME CANNOT TOUCH HER NOW.

1864 LATE SUMMER. OUT OF HIS BROTHER'S SHADOW, JOHN WILKES BOOTH'S STAR IS ON THE RISE...
HAMLET
THEATE
...AND SO IS BOOTH'S VALUE TO HIS CONFEDERATE NETWORK.
SAYS HERE THAT PRESIDENT LINCOLN'S A BIG THEATER FAN.
ROUND HOUSE
FINE
BEERS & SPIR
HEY!!
IT ALSO SAYS YOU ARE THE GREATEST ACTOR OF YOUR GENERATION...
...AND THAT LINCOLN IS GOING TO BE RE-ELECTED...
CAN'T BELIEVE EVERYTHING YOU READ IN THE PAPERS...
'CEPT THAT PART ABOUT ME!
WHAT'S THE NEWS FROM MONTREAL?
THE ST
YOU WANT TO KNOW THE PLAN?
I'M READY TO GO, JOHNNIE.
WELL, I COULD TELL YOU.
BUT THEN I'D HAVE TO KILL YOU, CLYDE.

DUTY CALLS ...
SURRATT'S BACK WITHIN THE WEEK.
!
!
EDWIN ?..
THANKS AGAIN, SIR ...
NOW, ELLA, WAIT!
JOHNNIE !!
OUT IN PUBLIC,
WITH A TROLLOP!
SHE'S A BARMAID!
FOR GOD'S SAKE, WHAT ABOUT LUCY?
KEEP HER OUT OF THIS!!
RPHY
BACCO
& FINEST
EPHANT
TONIC
DeKOPK
SOAP
DeKOPK
SOAP

OCTOBER 1864, THE SANITARY COMMISSION OFFICE
SO YOU WILL DO OUR BENEFIT?
THE WINTER GARDEN PROMISES TO DONATE ALL THE PROCEEDS ...
...IF YOU AND YOUR BROTHERS SIGN ON.
I'M READY!
TIME TO GET BACK ON STAGE!
I DON'T WANT TO RUSH YOU!
IT'S BEEN MONTHS, AND EDWINA'S DOING WELL AT MY MOTHER'S ...
I THINK JULIUS CAESAR IS A SPLENDID IDEA!
I CAN TACKLE BRUTUS IF JUNIUS PLAYS CAESAR.
AND JOHNNIE?
I'M NOT SURE IT'S A GOOD IDEA. THERE ARE THINGS ABOUT MY BROTHER YOU DON'T KNOW!
BUT IF YOU WERE TO ASK HIM...
I DON'T MIND ASKING, I JUST DON'T WANT YOU TO BE DISAPPOINTED ...
AND I WOULDN'T WANT YOUR FATHER TO GET THE WRONG IDEA.
YOU GET YOUR BROTHER TO PLAY MARC ANTONY AND I'LL TAKE CARE OF MY FATHER.

WHY CAN'T I GO WITH YOU TO NEW YORK ?
I'VE NEVER BEEN TO NEW YORK
I NEED YOU HERE, ELLA.
YOU'RE MY EYES AND EARS ...
...MY LIPS...
JUST SEEMS LIKE YOU HAVE YOUR MIND ON OTHER THINGS BESIDES THE UNDERGROUND, THESE DAYS !
I'LL BE BACK IN JUST A FEW DAYS.
WILL MISS HIGH AND MIGHTY BE IN NEW YORK ?
SHE'S THE ONE WHO ORGANIZED IT ALL WITH JUNIUS, EDWIN, AND ME.
I THOUGHT EDWIN WASN'T ACTING ANY-MORE!
HE'S A SHELL, A MERE SHADOW OF HIS FORMER SELF. I CAN'T BELIEVE SHE TALKED HIM INTO IT!
WELL,

... DON'T BE SURPRISED AT WHAT MIGHT BE WAITING FOR YOU WHEN YOU GET BACK!
WHAT DO YOU MEAN?
YOU KEEP SAYING WE HAVE TO DO SOMETHING ...
ESPECIALLY WITH THAT APE RE-ELECTED AND OUR NETWORK IN SHAMBLES! ...
CLYDE'S BEEN PUTTING TOGETHER A PLAN, JOHNNIE.
WHAT PLAN?
HE THINKS LINCOLN CAN BE HAULED OUT OF ONE OF THE BOXES AT THE THEATER ...
SNATCH HIM DURING A PLAY ...
ELLA, YOU MUST NEVER SPEAK OF SUCH THINGS!
CLYDE'S GOING TO GET US ALL THROWN INTO JAIL —OR WORSE
DON'T WORRY—
I'D DIE BEFORE GIVING ANYTHING AWAY.

NEW YORK CITY
NOV. 25, 18
BOOT
BROTHERS REUNI
ONE NIGHT ONLY!
William Shakesp
JULIUS CAES
NEWY
TER
OLD
EDWIN!
JUNIUS!
MOTHER!

MISS HALE, MISTER BOOTH: WELCOME TO DELMONICO'S!
IONICO'S

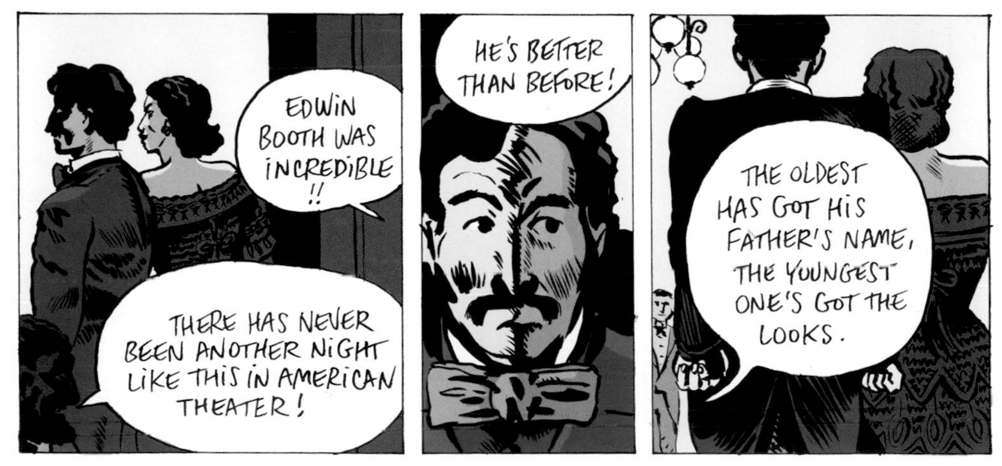
EDWIN BOOTH WAS INCREDIBLE !!
THERE HAS NEVER BEEN ANOTHER NIGHT LIKE THIS IN AMERICAN THEATER!
HE'S BETTER THAN BEFORE!
THE OLDEST HAS GOT HIS FATHER'S NAME, THE YOUNGEST ONE'S GOT THE LOOKS.

AND THE ONE IN THE MIDDLE'S GOT ALL THE TALENT!
I HEAR HE'S DOING "HAMLET" NEXT YEAR.
TONIGHT MIGHT ADD TO EDWIN'S PROBLEMS.
PEOPLE EXPECT HIM TO GO BACK ON STAGE!
WOULDN'T IT BE WONDERFUL?
I'D LIKE TO PROPOSE A TOAST TO OUR GOOD FRIENDS AT THE SANITARY COMMISSION WHO MADE THIS NIGHT POSSIBLE...
BUT MOST ESPECIALLY TO THE LOVELY LUCY HALE, WHO PREVAILED ON ME TO TAKE ON THE ROLE OF BRUTUS...
HEAR!
HEAR!!
HIP HIP! HOORAY!!
...FOR THIS GLORIOUS CAUSE!
CHEERS!
JOLLY GOOD!
LET'S HEAR IT FOR LUCY!!!
TO MY MOTHER MARY ANN, WHO WAS MY FATHER'S MAINSTAY DURING HIS LONG AND ILLUSTROUS CAREER!
AND I WANT TO CONCLUDE BY SHARING SOME NEWS...
...SOME OF YOU MAY KNOW...

AFTER THE DEATH OF MY OWN BELOVED MARY, I SWORE OFF PERFORMING...
"BUT THIS EVENING MARKS NOT ONLY THE LARGEST SINGLE DONATION TO THE UNION CAUSE,"
LET'S HEAR IT FOR THE UNION!!
"BUT THE END OF MY EXILE FROM THE STAGE."
"I HAVE MADE PLANS TO RETURN TO THE BOARDS"
?
"THE FIRST WEEK OF JANUARY."
!
SLAM!
THAT'S TREMENDOUS!!
YOU HAVE MADE ME SO VERY HAPPY!
OH, EDWIN!
I'VE NEGLECTED YOU ALL EVENING, JOHNNIE, BUT THE BALL IS OVER, AND NOW I'M ALL YOURS!

NOW THAT EDWIN'S GONE...
...YOU HAVE TIME FOR ME?
WHAT?
YOU WERE BOTH PLOTTING ALL ALONG.
THAT'S THE WHISKEY TALKING ...
!
DON'T YOU REALIZE WHAT YOU'VE DONE?
I'VE JUST HAD THE MOST SUCCESSFUL NIGHT OF MY LIFE— CAN'T YOU BE HAPPY FOR ME?! CAN'T YOU SHARE THE LIMELIGHT FOR ONCE IN YOUR LIFE?
I'VE HAD TO SHARE EVERYTHING I'VE EVER WORKED FOR —EVERYTHING I EVER DREAMED OF!
THE NEXT MORNING, AT THE HALE HOME
IT WON'T BE ANNOUNCED FOR A FEW DAYS...
...BUT I'VE JUST HEARD YOU'LL BE INVITED TO SERVE ON THE PLANNING COMMITTEE FOR THE INAUGURATION ...
OH, PAPA, I CAN'T BELIEVE IT !!!
IT'S WORTH EVERY PENNY IF YOU PROMISE TO START SMILING AGAIN.

THIS IS OUR CHANCE TO SHOW THE WHITE HOUSE WHAT YOU CAN DO!
WHAT WE CAN DO!
AT THE SANITARY COMMISSION OFFICE
I GUESS ABSENCE MAKES THE HEART GROW FONDER?
IF YOU EVER GO AWAY AGAIN FOR SUCH A LONG TIME, I SWEAR I'LL LEARN TO LIVE WITHOUT YOU!
NEVER ...
LOOK ...
... WHAT I BROUGHT YOU!
IT'S BEAUTIFUL, JOHN, BUT YOU SHOULDN'T HAVE!
DID YOU GET A CHANCE TO TALK TO YOUR FATHER?
SO YOU HAVEN'T TOLD HIM YET.
HE'S SO BUSY NOW.
AND I'M SO IMPATIENT.

Chapter 5

Wherein:

- Lucy Hale receives a notable invitation, and confusion ensues.

- With Lincoln on the verge of a second term and the tide of war turning against the confederates, Booth's shadow associates become increasingly desperate.

- Too busy with his conspiracies to attend Edwin's 100th performance of *Hamlet*, Booth sends Ella in his place. An awkward meeting ensues between Ella and Lucy Hale.

ONE FLAG ONE COU
ONE DESTINY
REPUBLI
EADQUA
EDWIN BOOTH as AMLE
DON'T MISS THE GREATEST ACTOR ALIVE TODAY
A FEW DAYS BEFORE CHRISTMAS 1864. THE HALES' PARLOR
AND SO MOTHER'S HAVING FRIENDS OVER...
...AND WE THOUGHT IF YOU AND YOUR FATHER COULD JOIN US...

MY MOTHER AND I WOULD BE HONORED.
MY FATHER ...
THEY SAY ...
WHAT ABOUT THE PRESIDENT?
MY FATHER SAYS GENERAL SHERMAN MAY GIVE US SOMETHING TO CELEBRATE THIS CHRISTMAS.
I'M ...
I'M JUST GLAD YOU ARE FREE ON SATURDAY EVENING.
I DIDN'T SAY I WAS FREE, ROBERT...
DON'T GO SPREADING RUMORS ABOUT ME SITTING HOME ALONE ON A SATURDAY NIGHT!
I DIDN'T MEAN...

I WILL REARRANGE MY SCHEDULE FOR AN INVITATION TO THE WHITE HOUSE.
UNTIL SATURDAY ...
CATO?
YES, MISS LUCY?
TAKE A MESSAGE TO THE ROUND HOUSE TAVERN FOR ME.
I CAN'T DO THAT, MISS LUCY.
!?
THE ROUND HOUSE IS NO PLACE FOR COLOREDS THESE DAYS— KIDNAPPINGS AND ALL...
KIDNAPPINGS?
SECESSIONISTS STEAL COLORED FOLK AND SELL THEM INTO VIRGINIA.
I HAD NO IDEA!!!
THE CHESAPEAKE IS FULL OF BOATS – SLAVES PADDLING NORTH TO GET FREE - WHILE DISTRICT BLACKS GETTING STOLEN. I'M NOT PLANNING TO BE ONE OF THEM...
...BUT IF THIS LETTER IS FOR MR. BOOTH
IT IS...
I'LL TAKE IT TO THE FORD THEATER, WHERE HE PICKS UP HIS MAIL ...
THANK YOU, CATO!

THIS IS FOR Mr. BOOTH, FROM MISS HALE...
HUH? Mr. BOOTH? RIGHT.
HERE'S YOUR MAIL, EDWIN.
THANK YOU, NED!
THE DAY BEFORE CHRISTMAS EVE, SATURDAY
HAVE A GOOD HOLIDAY, JOHNNIE!
OH, I PLAN TO, NED...
... THIS IS GOING TO BE THE BEST CHRISTMAS EVER
DONG!
DONG!
?!
NO ONE'S AT HOME, SIR.
I'M HERE TO SEE MISS HALE!
AIN'T NOBODY HERE!

LISTEN, YOU IGNORANT BABOON:
I DON'T GIVE A DAMN WHAT HER FATHER HAS TOLD YOU...
I'M HERE...
TO SEE LUCY!
LUCY!
LUCY!
DON'T MAKE ME CALL THE LAW ON YOU, Mr. BOOTH!
THEY'VE GONE TO THE WHITE HOUSE.
THAT HAD BETTER BE THE TRUTH!
...OR THIS IS THE LAST LIE YOU'LL EVER TELL!
YEAAAH!
FORD THEATER
STAGE DOOR
NO ENTRY

JOHNNIE ?
SORRY MISS TURNER, HE'S GONE FOR THE NIGHT.
LEFT IN A PRETTY GOOD MOOD ...
HE DID, DID HE ?
HOPE YOU CATCH UP TO HIM ...
YOU KNOW JOHNNIE. THERE'S NO USE TRYING UNTIL HE'S READY TO GET CAUGHT.
LATER THAT NIGHT
THE ROUND HOUSE
MY USUAL.
QUIET NIGHT. MOST FOLKS AT HOME WITH THEIR FAMILIES ...
OR WHAT'S LEFT OF 'EM.
AREN'T YOUR PEOPLE IN MARYLAND ?
ALL GONE TO NEW YORK... ...TO MY BROTHER EDWIN'S.
NEW YORK'S NOT A LONG WAY OFF, JOHN...
WHERE IS ELLA ?
HER FOLKS ARE DEAD...

... SINCE HER BROTHER DIED AT ANTIETAM, WE'RE ALL SHE'S GOT.
I KNOW ALL THAT!
I MEAN: HAVE YOU SEEN HER TONIGHT?
SHE CAME IN WITH A FELLA FROM THE TREASURY DEPARTMENT.
THEY WENT UPSTAIRS.
'COURSE IT'S TRUE!
... OUR GUY SAW THE TELEGRAM!
WHAT'S THIS ALL ABOUT?
CLYDE SAYS THE REBS HAVE ABANDONED SAVANNAH!
CLYDE, HOW MANY TIMES HAVE I TOLD YOU TO KEEP YOUR MOUTH SHUT?!
HE SEEN THE TELEGRAM!!
KEEP YOUR VOICE DOWN ANYWAY!
SOUNDS LIKE A LOT OF YANKEE COCK AND BULL!
SPEAKING OF YANKEE COCK...
SLAP!
POUR TWO FINGERS OF YOUR BEST WHISKEY, AND...

YOU HAVE TO TAKE THAT DRINK WITH YOU...
I'M NOT GOING ANYWHERE!
YOUR WIFE JUST SENT A MESSENGER AROUND LOOKING FOR YOU.
MY WIFE?!
YOUR WIFE ?
WHAT DO YOU MEAN, DECEIVING THIS LADY ?
YOU MUST BE PULLING MY LEG— THIS IS NO LADY!
WATCH YOUR MOUTH, MISTER!
WHAT'S GOTTEN INTO YOU, BOYS ?
THE REBS HAVE DESERTED SAVANNAH!
WHAT?
TIME IS RUNNING OUT, ELLA.
AT THE WHITE HOUSE PARLOR, LATER THAT EVENING
TO SHERMAN'S SPLENDID CHRISTMAS PRESENT, Mr. PRESIDENT!

SHHH, CLOSE YOUR EYES...
EARLY JANUARY 1865
THE ROUND HOUSE
FINE BEERS & WHI
ELLA IS AT THE PHARMACY.
SHE SAID GO AHEAD AND HAVE SUPPER WITHOUT HER...
WHY DIDN'T SHE SEND FOR DAVID HEROLD?

SHE WANTED IT BEFORE THE MIDDLE OF NEXT WEEK!?
JOHN WILKES BOOTH?
WHO WANTS TO KNOW?
?...
TELL ELLA NOT TO WAIT.
ARE YOU SURE? I'VE NEVER SEEN THESE FELLAS BEFORE!
YOU HAVEN'T SEEN US AT ALL...
IF YOU KNOW WHAT'S GOOD FOR YOU.
SECURITY'S VITAL IN THESE DARK DAYS ...

WE MUST HAVE A PLAN BEFORE THE INAUGURATION.
SO REMOVING STOVE PIPE HAS BEEN APPROVED ...
YOUR NEXT CONTACT —CODE NAME BRUTUS— WILL BE IN TOUCH. YOU AND YOU ALONE HAVE BEEN SELECTED.
CONFIDE IN NO ONE OR THERE WILL BE CONSEQUENCES ...
I UNDERSTAND.
I HOPE YOU DO, Mr. BOOTH, WE ARE NOT PLAY-ACTING!
YOU CAN TELL BRUTUS ...
TELL HIM YOURSELF!
... I'VE NEVER MET HIM.
REMEMBER, TELL NO ONE ...
IT'S VICTORY OR DEATH!
... VICTORY OR DEATH ...
LUCY!
LUCY, IT'S ME!
I MUST SEE YOU!
?!
JOHNNIE!
I THOUGHT WE AGREED ...
I MUST SEE YOU NOW!

STOP!
I'LL COME DOWN.
WE AGREED LAST WEEK THAT WE WOULD KEEP OUR ENGAGEMENT SECRET!
... WE WOULDN'T SEE ONE ANOTHER UNTIL I HAD TIME TO TALK WITH MY FATHER...
HAVE YOU?
I HAVEN'T HAD A CHANCE...
JUST GET IT OVER WITH...
IT DOESN'T MATTER WHEN YOU TELL HIM!
IT MATTERS TO ME!
I WANT YOU TO WEAR MY RING!
I AM WEARING IT NEXT TO MY HEART.
SPEAK TO YOUR FATHER!
SOON, I PROMISE... NOW GO!
WHEN CAN WE BE TOGETHER AGAIN?
I'LL LEAVE THE BACK DOOR TO THE COMMISSION OFFICE UNLOCKED...
COME AFTER FIVE TOMORROW.

INAUGURATION DAY
THE HERAL
INAUGURAT

THE ROUND HOUSE
FINE BEERS & WHISKEYS
CLOSED
JOHNNIE SAID TO TELL YOU...
I KNOW, I KNOW: HE'LL SEE ME LATER!
HE'S BEEN SAYING THAT FOR WEEKS NOW...
HE'S BUSIER THAN A BEE IN A CLOVER, ELLA. AT SURRATTVILLE YESTERDAY AND BACK FROM BALTIMORE ONLY THE DAY BEFORE!!!
JOHNNIE'S BUSY, ALL RIGHT...
...BUT I HAVE A MESSAGE HE'LL WANT—FROM THE COWPOKES.
COWPOKES?
YOU REMEMBER THOSE FOUR TOUGHS WHO CAME IN AND TOOK HIM AWAY?
I DON'T KNOW WHAT YOU'RE TALKING ABOUT.
GOT A MESSAGE FOR YOU, JOHNNIE!
WILKES, THERE'S SOME BIG SHINDIG TONIGHT OVER AT GROVER'S THEATER!

YOUR BROTHER IS DOING HIS ONE-HUNDREDTH PERFORMANCE OF HAMLET.
WILL YOU TAKE ME WITH YOU?
I'M NOT SURE, ELLA.
AFTER YOU COME BACK FROM LOOKING AT THE HORSE...
WHAT HORSE?
FELLA TOLD ME YOU WANTED TO LOOK AT A STALLION CALLED **BRUTUS**.
?!
WHAT'S THIS ABOUT BRUTUS?
HE TOLD ME TO TELL YOU TO COME ALONG TONIGHT TO ROCK CREEK AT SUNSET.
ANYTHING ELSE?
SAID TO COME ALONE ...
... AND HE'D BRING THE PICNIC THIS TIME...
THANK YOU, ELLA! ...
... YOU DON'T KNOW...
A PICNIC WITH A HORSE?
... WHAT THIS MEANS TO ME!
BUT WHAT ABOUT ...
... THE TICKET ?

GROVER'S THEATER
GOOD EVENING.
!
DO WE HAVE THE RIGHT BOX?
I'M A GUEST OF Mr. BOOTH'S.
AH, WE WERE EXPECTING HIS BROTHER.
HIS BROTHER'S PLAYING HAMLET TONIGHT... I'M JOHNNIE'S GUEST.
THE CURTAIN'S ABOUT TO GO UP!
CLAP!
CLAP!
CLAP!
CLAP!
CLAP!
?

CLYDE!?!
"THAT SKULL HAD A TONGUE IN IT, AND COULD SING ONCE:
HOW THE KNAVE JOWLS IT TO THE GROUND,
AS IF IT WERE CAIN'S JAWBONE,
THAT DID THE FIRST MURDER!"
WHAT WERE YOU DOING AT SURRATTVILLE?
WHO'S YOUR CONTACT THERE?
I HAVE NO IDEA...
...WHAT YOU'RE...
"

...TALKIN' ABOUT!...
WE'RE NOT LEAVING HERE UNTIL YOU TELL US WHAT WE WANT TO KNOW.
I DON'T KNOW ANYTHING!
I'M JUST AN ACTOR!
OOW!
...
A TRAITOR WORKING FOR JEFF DAVIS!
WHO'S BRUTUS?
I DON'T KNOW ANY BRUTUS.
!...
IT'S TOO CROWDED, PAPA!
WE'LL PAY OUR RESPECTS AND THEN WE CAN GO.
THERE SHE IS!!

CONGRATULATIONS, EDWIN!
SHE RESTORED MY FAITH IN MYSELF...
SHE REUNITED ME WITH MY BROTHER...
AND BY THE WAY, WHERE IS JOHNNIE?
HE WAS, UH, DETAINED. ...
...AND GAVE HIS TICKET AWAY.
I DON'T UNDERSTAND...
LUCY HAS A TOUCH OF NEURALGIA... I MUST BE GETTING HER HOME.
WHY, OF COURSE!
I...
...I UNDERSTAND ...

NOW YOU'LL GET A CHANCE TO DIE FOR HONOR, REB!
WHICH ONE OF YOUR GIRLFRIENDS KEEPS THE CIPHER?
THEY KNOW NOTHING, DO YOU HEAR ME?
THAT LITTLE ELLA... WOULDN'T MIND TRYING TO SNEAK A PEEK UNDER HER... PILLOW.
OR VISITING THE SENATOR'S DAUGHTER ...
I ALREADY TOLD YOU. LUCY KNOWS NOTHING!
LAST CHANCE. TELL US RIGHT NOW AND WE WON'T HARM THEM.
YOU'VE GOT TO BELIEVE ME!
YEEEHAP!
I'M SURE THERE'S AN EXPLANATION WHY JOHN WAS CALLED AWAY.
AND SENT A STREETWALKER IN HIS PLACE!
YOU DON'T KNOW ...
I KNOW YOU DON'T DESERVE THIS KIND OF TREATMENT!

IF YOU LOVE ME, PAPA, YOU'LL STAY OUT OF THIS!
I CANNOT SIT BY, ESPECIALLY NOW...
I WAS HOPING TO TELL YOU UNDER HAPPIER CIR-CUMSTANCES...
...BUT PRESIDENT LINCOLN HAS ASKED ME TO BE HIS AMBASSADOR TO SPAIN.
PAPA! THAT'S WONDERFUL! SPAIN!
WHY, THAT'S MORE THAN WE EVER HOPED FOR!!
I'M SO GLAD YOU'RE PLEASED AND NOW, MORE THAN EVER, YOU NEED TO GET AWAY!
I'M NOT SURE...
YOU ALWAYS WANTED TO SEE THE CONTINENT!
YOU DESERVE A HOLIDAY FROM HOSPITAL WARDS.
I KNOW PAPA, BUT...
YOU WOULD BE PRESENTED AT COURT!
BUT, PAPA...
JUST SLEEP ON IT FOR NOW — WE'LL DISCUSS IT IN THE MORNING.

GUESS WE MADE PRETTY GOOD YANKEES!
HAD YOU FOOLED!
...
WELCOME TO PRESIDENT DAVIS'S SECRET SERVICE!
... CAN... ...CAN I HAVE MY WEAPON BACK?
NOW THAT YOU UNDERSTAND FULLY OUR NEED FOR SECURITY...
!
YOU NEARLY KILLED ME TONIGHT!
WE CAN'T TAKE ANY CHANCES.
COMRADES IN RICHMOND AND MONTREAL ASSURE ME THAT LINCOLN IS VULNERABLE...
...BUT SO ARE WE, Mr. BOOTH, SO PLEASE FOR-GIVE THE PRECAUTIONS!
I'VE BEEN TELLING YOU FOR MONTHS WE NEED TO GET LINCOLN!
...BUT NOW IT'S TOO LATE!!! HE KEEPS A GUARD ALL THE WAY TO THE SOLDIERS HOME.

IT'S NEVER TOO LATE FOR GREATNESS, SURELY YOUR CAREER HAS TAUGHT YOU THAT!
THE IDEA OF SNATCHING HIM FROM THE THEATER IS INTRIGUING...
THAT WOULD NEVER WORK, AND...
...HOW DID YOU—
YOU WERE BETRAYED.
CLYDE ...
YOU DIDN'T HAVE TO KILL HIM.
THEN I'VE MISJUDGED YOU ... AND YOUR ABILITY TO SERVE.
DIDN'T I PROVE MYSELF TONIGHT?
YOU MUST NOT JUST BE PREPARED TO DIE, BUT BE WILLING TO KILL FOR THE CAUSE.
I'M READY.
LET'S PUT THAT FAMED MEMORY TO THE TEST.
OUR OPERATION'S CODE IS "TYRANNUS" ...
TYRANNUS...

Chapter 6

Wherein:

- The neglected Ella meets an honest soldier, and Booth severs his relations with Lucy.
- The shadow conspirators meet a final time at Mrs. Surratt's boarding house, and Booth says his last goodbyes.
- The deed is done: With pistol in one hand and knife in the other, John Wilkes Booth becomes a murderer.

BANG!

ELLA, ALONE
LEAVE ME ALONE!
HEY, THERE!
YOU GOT NO CALL TO INTERFERE!
LET HER GO.
YOU... YOU WANT...
... HER FOR YOURSELF!
GO SLEEP IT OFF!

YOU GOT NO CALL, BUT GO AHEAD,
GO AHEAD! ...
GUNS &c
WEDDING GOW
COLD BEER
... AND TAKE HER FOR YOURSELF!
THANK YOU, SOLDIER!
SORRY, MA'AM!
THANK YOU FOR YOUR CONCERN, PRIVATE ...?
PRIVATE HARRIS, MA'AM, BUT YOU CAN CALL ME JOE.
WELL, JOE, I'M WALKING HOME FROM THE THEATER.
ARE YOU AN ACTRESS?
HAHA! OH MY GOODNESS, NO!
?
PERHAPS I MIGHT CALL ON YOU AGAIN ...

WE HAVE MEN FROM MONTREAL TO MEXICO, IN NEW YORK, PHILADELPHIA,
AND RIGHT HERE, IN WASHINGTON.
MEN OF VALOR WORKING FOR SOUTHERN INDEPENDENCE, TO RECLAIM OUR RIGHTS.
LAUNDR
WE PLEDGE OUR HONOR!
OUR LIVES!
WELCOME TO OUR GLORIOUS CAUSE!
VICTORY OR DEATH!
YOU MUST NOT CONFIDE IN ELLA TURNER ...
ELLA'S LOYAL TO THE CAUSE!
SHE'S LOYAL TO YOU — BUT WORKS FOR WHOEVER CAN PAY.
OUR OPERATION MUST BE TOTALLY SECURE.
YES, OF COURSE.
LET HER KEEP YOUR BED WARM, BUT NOT A WHISPER ABOUT TYRANNUS.

AT THE NATIONAL HOTEL, THE NEXT MORNING
The Examiner
RICHMOND CAPTURED
EDWIN!
I'M SORRY ABOUT MISSING YOUR PERFORMANCE!
THAT'S QUITE ALL RIGHT.
BUT IT'S ANOTHER MATTER ENTIRELY TO SEND A WHORE TO SIT IN MY BOX.
SHE'S NOT A WHORE!!!
YOU SHOULD HAVE SEEN THE SENATOR'S FACE... THIS HAS GOT TO STOP OR ELSE!
WHAT? YOU'LL TELL MOTHER?
WHAT GOOD WOULD THAT DO?
SHE'S LET YOU HAVE YOUR WAY FROM THE DAY YOU WERE BORN.
I HAVE A RICH, BEAUTIFUL WOMAN WHO WANTS TO BE MY WIFE; AND MY NOTICES RIVAL YOURS!
YES.

YES - HERE'S A REAL CHANCE FOR HAPPINESS,
AN OPPORTUNITY TO CREATE A THEATRICAL DYNASTY,
AND YOU'RE FRITTERING IT AWAY...
JOHN, PLEASE, THE WAR WILL BE OVER SOON!
WE'LL SEE ABOUT THAT!
AT LEAST YOU WERE CLEVER ENOUGH TO SIT IT OUT!
TAKE THAT BACK!
?
!!
JOHN?...
WHAT ARE YOU DOING HERE?
JOHN,
WE HAVE TO TALK.
...AT MY BROTHER'S HOTEL?!
DON'T BE RIDICULOUS!
STOP YOUR INSULTS!

I'LL LEAVE YOU TWO TO BE ALONE.
STOP BEHAVING LIKE A CHILD!
EDWIN, YOU'RE BLEEDING!
JOHN! FETCH A DOCTOR!!
FROM THIS DAY FORWARD, MISS HALE, I RELEASE YOU FROM ANY OBLIGATION.
...
HAVE YOU TAKEN LEAVE OF YOUR SENSES?
FOR GOD'S SAKE, GET YOUR BROTHER A DOCT—
LEE'S SURRENDED!
?

THE REBS ARE FINALLY WHIPPED!!!
WE CANNOT MEET HERE AGAIN.
Mrs SURRATT'S BOARDING HOUSE
NO VACANCIES
WHERE ARE WE GOING TO FIND ENOUGH FRESH HORSES?
I'LL TAKE CARE OF EVERYTHING — JUST BE PREPARED FOR THE DAY OF RECKONING,
AND UPON MY SIGNAL,
BE WHERE I'VE TOLD YOU, WHEN I'VE TOLD YOU!
WE'LL BE READY ... BUT WHEN...
SOON,
VERY SOON...

... BUT WE MUST KEEP OUR PLANS TO OURSELVES.
KNOCK KNOCK!
?!!
WHO IS IT?
CAN YOU GET THE DOOR, Mr.... "Mr. BOYD"?
I THOUGHT YOU GENTLEMEN MIGHT LIKE SOME REFRESHMENTS.
THE PACKAGE IS READY... I HEARD FROM...
NO NAMES!
WE CANNOT RISK ANY DISCOVERY, ESPECIALLY NOW.
YES OF COURSE!
"Mr. BOYD."
THANK YOU, Mrs. SURRATT!
YOU KNOW, I'M ALONE THIS EVENING ...
I'LL TRY TO COME BACK LATER ...
YOU ARE BEING OF SUCH SERVICE TO OUR CAUSE, DEAR LADY!
WOULD ANYONE LIKE MORE CAKE?

WASHINGTON STAAARR, WASHINGTON STAAAR!
VOLUN
WAN
RICHMOND OCCUPIED!
THANK YOU, SIR!
LEE ON THE RUN!
DAVIS FLEES!
UNION VICTORY

COME TO BED ...
APRIL 13th 1865.
WHO CAN SLEEP WHILE THAT BABOON LINCOLN MEASURES HIS HEAD FOR A CROWN?
YOU SHOULD HAVE HEARD HIM — GIVE THE NIGGER THE VOTE...
WE'LL SEE ABOUT THAT!
JOHNNIE, YOU HAVEN'T HAD A NIGHT'S SLEEP SINCE RICHMOND FELL!
I'M LEAVING TOWN...
WHEN?
SOON.
I WANT TO GO WITH YOU!
YOU CAN'T JUST YET.
"FOR ME,"
"DEAREST MOTHER, I HAVE NOT A SINGLE SELFISH MOTIVE TO SPUR ME ON TO THIS..."
BUT I'LL SEND FOR YOU ... SOON...
WHEN IT IS SAFE.
PLEASE, ELLA, DON'T FAIL ME NOW!
... "NOTHING SAVE THE SACRED DUTY I FEEL I OWE THE CAUSE..."
WHEN HAVE I EVER LET YOU DOWN?

I'M LEAVING YOU SOME LETTERS TO POST FOR ME.
SEND THEM ONCE I'VE LEFT TOWN.
"TO THE NATIONAL INTELLIGENCER:"
"FOR A LONG TIME I HAVE DEVOTED MY ENERGIES, MY TIME AND MONEY TO THE ACCOMPLISHMENT OF..."
"...A CERTAIN END."
"THE MOMENT HAS NOW ARRIVED WHEN I MUST CHANGE MY PLANS."
"MANY WILL BLAME ME FOR WHAT I AM ABOUT TO DO,"
"BUT POSTERITY, I AM SURE, WILL JUSTIFY ME."
"MY DEAREST LUCY, I KNOW IT HAS HURT YOU DEEPLY FOR ME TO PRETEND THAT I DO NOT CARE FOR YOU..."
"BUT ..."

"IT WAS BEST FOR US BOTH"
"THAT YOU HAD NO INKLING OF MY ROLE IN THE UPRISING."
Mrs Mary Booth 46 W. 11st. Ne
National Intelli
Mr. Edwin c/o The
WHAT TIME IS IT ?
IT'S EARLY, GO BACK TO SLEEP!
THE HORSE MUST BE WAITING FOR ME IN BAPTIST ALLEY.
APRIL 14 1865, WASHINGTON, GOOD FRIDAY
?
THERE GOES THE PRESIDENT ...
WE MUST BE MORE CHEERFUL. BETWEEN THE LOSS OF OUR DARLING WILLIE AND THE WAR, WE HAVE BOTH BEEN VERY MISERABLE.

OHIO'S NOT THE WEST ANYMORE, ELLA. THIS COUNTRY'S HEADED ALL THE WAY TO THE PACIFIC, ONCE THEY GET THE RAILROAD BUILT!
BENEFIT!
LAST NIGHT
LAURA KEENE
YOU MAKE IT SOUND SO EXCITING, JOE!
IT IS EXCITING. AND YOU AND I CAN BE PART OF IT.
THE WHITE HOUSE
MOTHER HAD A HEADACHE BUT FATHER WANTED TO GO.
YOU SHOULD HAVE GONE WITH THEM!
I'VE SEEN LAURA KEENE BEFORE, AND...
I WANTED TO BE WITH YOU...

FORD'S THEATER

AT THAT MOMENT

KNOCK! KNOCK!
... DELIVERY FOR SECRETARY SEWARD!

"YOU WILL PLEASE RECOLLECT YOU ARE ADRESSING MY DAUGHTER, AND IN MY PRESENCE."
OUR AMERICAN
COUSIN
SOLD OU
"YES, I'M OFFERING HER MY HEART AND HAND JUST AS SHE WANTS THEM WITH NOTHING IN 'EM."
"AUGUSTA, DEAR, TO YOUR ROOM!"
"YES, MA, THE NASTY BEAST!"
"I AM AWARE, Mr. TRENCHARD,
"YOU ARE NOT USED TO THE MANNERS OF GOOD SOCIETY,
"AND THAT, ALONE,
"WILL EXCUSE THE IMPERTINENCE OF WHICH YOU HAVE BEEN GUILTY..."

"DON'T KNOW THE MANNERS OF GOOD SOCIETY, EH?
"WELL, I GUESS I KNOW ENOUGH TO TURN YOU INSIDE OUT, OLD GAL!
YOU
SOCKDOLOGIZING
OLD
MAN-TRAP!"
BANG!

SIC
TYRANNUS!

I'M SORRY, ROBERT.
NO
NOT AT ALL, PLEASE FORGIVE ME!
IT'S JUST THAT I'M HAVING SOME TROUBLE SORTING THINGS OUT.
THIS WAY, DOC, QUICK!!!
MAKE WAY, FOR MAKE WAY!
DAVY.
JOHNNIE.

I'D LOVE TO COME BACK...
...FOR MORE LESSONS...
OF COURSE! I HOPE YOU DON'T THINK
NOT AT ALL, ROBERT!
SLAM
WE HAVE TO SECURE THE WHITE HOUSE!
I'LL TAKE YOU HOME.
SIR...
WE HAVE INSTRUCTIONS TO KEEP YOU HERE – UNTIL WE GET WORD.
I INSIST...
SIR!
THERE HAS BEEN AN ATTACK ON SECRETARY SEWARD'S HOUSE!
JOHNNIE!!

GOOD GOD!
BROKEN ...
I MUST GET TO MY FATHER!
THIS WAY, MISS HALE!
..., DON'T KNOW HOW MUCH LONGER I CAN GO ON, DAVY!
WE'RE ALMOST THERE, JOHNNIE. HANG ON UNTIL WE GET TO A DOCTOR!
THE PRESIDENT'S BEEN SHOT!
WHAT'S THAT?
WHAT ARE YOU TALKING ABOUT?
LINCOLN WAS SHOT!!!

SEWARD WAS KILLED IN HIS BED AND REBS ARE EVERYWHERE!
THE WAR'S STARTING ALL OVER AGAIN!
I'VE DONE EVERYTHING I CAN FOR HIM.
SAVE HIM, YOU MUST SAVE HIM!
TAKE THAT WOMAN OUT OF HERE ...
OH JOHNNIE!
The National Intel
Agency
284 Gre
Wester
never
... HOW COULD YOU?
NOW HE BELONGS TO THE AGES.

Chapter 7

Wherein:

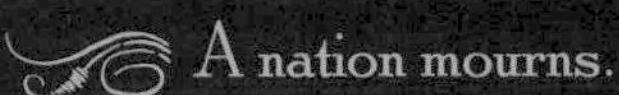

- A nation mourns.

- Booth, aided by the loyal Davy, flees south, finding aid and allies—both knowing and ignorant of his crime—at every turn.

- Ella, the only member of the Round House gang to remain at large, witnesses her fellow conspirators apprehended—and attempts to do herself an injury.

Dearest

MARYLAND
CAN I GET YOU ANYTHING ELSE, Mr. TYSON?
Nooo.

THANKS,,, MY BROTHER WILL BE FINE NOW.

MY HUSBAND SAYS HE MUST STAY OFF HIS LEG FOR IT TO HEAL PROPERLY.

WE'LL BE GOING TO A PLACE WHERE HE CAN REST.

« SURGITE MORTUI, VENITE AD JUDICIUM! »

AT THE HALES', TWO DAYS LATER
AND YOU PROMISED ME YOU WOULD NOT READ THE PAPERS, LUCY...
THE COUNTRY HAS GONE MAD.
The Messenger
ANY GOOD-LOOKING MAN IS LIKELY TO GET ARRESTED!
EVERYONE'S CLAIMING THEY'VE SPOTTED JOHN WILKES BOOTH.
I TOLD YOU **NEVER** TO SPEAK THAT NAME AGAIN!
BUT JOHN DIDN'T DO THIS, PAPA! I KNOW HE DIDN'T! HE CAN'T ABIDE VIOLENCE!
WE HAVE BEEN OVER THIS AGAIN AND AGAIN, MY DEAR GIRL. WHAT ABOUT THE EYE-WITNESSES AT THE THEATER?
THEY COULD BE MISTAKEN!
WHY HASN'T HE COME FORWARD IF HE'S INNOCENT?
DON'T EXCITE YOURSELF!
THERE'S A LYNCH MOB AFTER HIM!!!

YOU BURNED ALL HIS LETTERS!
I HAD TO, LUCY.
EDWIN BOOTH'S AT THE DOOR, SENATOR, AND ASKS IF HE MIGHT SPEAK WITH YOU.
EDWIN!
I'VE BEEN TRAVELING ALL DAY...
MOTHER INSISTED THAT I COME TO WASHINGTON, SHE IS BESIDE HERSELF. I WANTED TO ASSURE YOU THAT I HAD NO IDEA ABOUT JOHN'S PLOT.
IT'S ALL A MISTAKE!
MAYBE YOU CAN TALK SOME SENSE INTO HER...
LUCY, MY BROTHER HAS DONE THIS TERRIBLE THING.
IT CAN'T BE TRUE.
SOLDIERS AT THE DOOR, SENATOR, SAYING THEY HAVE A WARRANT...

A WARRANT?
SORRY, SENATOR, BUT WE HAVE ORDERS TO APPREHEND THIS MAN, AND ANYONE HE CONTACTS...
OF COURSE, OF COURSE!
WE'LL COOPERATE FULLY, SERGEANT.
SENATOR, I'M SO VERY SORRY: I WOULDN'T HAVE COME, HAD I KNOWN...
I'LL GET MY HAT, SERGEANT, BUT PLEASE LEAVE MY DAUGHTER OUT OF THIS.
MY ORDERS ARE...
CAN SHE REMAIN UNDER HOUSE ARREST...
...UNTIL I GET THIS STRAIGHTENED OUT?
FINE
I'LL POST GUARDS.
COME ALONG...
I HAD NO IDEA...

DO NOT SPEAK TO ANYONE UNTIL I RETURN.
CATO, COME WITH ME!
HOURS LATER
?
BUT I DON'T UNDERSTAND, I THOUGHT YOU WERE LETTING ME GO?!
FOR YOUR OWN SAFETY,
?
YOU NEED TO WEAR THIS DISGUISE...
TO GET TO THE HOTEL.
MY MEN WILL ESCORT YOU.
FOR THE TIME BEING, YOU MUST NOT USE THE NAME BOOTH.
?!
THE ROUND HOUSE

POLICE
LET US AT 'EM!!
GO HOME!
JOHN WILKES BOOTH IS NOT HERE, I TELL YOU!
YOU CAUGHT HIM IN A BROTHEL!
IF WE HAD HIM YOU'D HEAR ABOUT HIM SOON ENOUGH!
JOHN WILKES BOOTH REMAINS AT LARGE!!
BUT I HASTEN TO REMIND YOU OF THE BOUNTY ON HIS HEAD!
AYE! FIFTY THOUSAND!
THE GOVERNMENT HAS RAISED THE REWARD TO ONE HUNDRED THOUSAND DOLLARS FOR BOOTH...
...AND FIFTY THOUSAND FOR ANYONE WHO CONSPIRED IN THE ATTACK ON SECRETARY SEWARD!
IN THE MARYLAND BACK COUNTRY

IT'S ME!
GOT YOU FRESH HORSES.
YOU CAN COME OUT NOW! IT'S SAFE...
WELL ...
I WOULDN'T GO SO FAR AS ALL THAT.
Mr.... JONES,
OUR GRATITUDE FOR ALL YOU'RE DOING FOR YOUR COUNTRY.
IT'S AN HONOR TO MEET YOU, SIR!
DID YOU BRING ANY NEWS?
HAVE THERE BEEN UPRISINGS? HAS IT BEGUN?
I WOULD HAVE THOUGHT THAT BY NOW SOUTHERN PATRIOTS WOULD HAVE RISEN UP!
WE CAN'T RIGHTLY WAIT FOR THAT, SIR.
THE COUNTRYSIDE IS CRAWLING WITH FEDS!
WE NEED TO REACH ZEKIAH SWAMPS BEFORE NIGHTFALL.

DAMN! SEWARD SURVIVED LEWIS'S ATTACK...
...BUT LEWIS GOT AWAY...
SORRY, SIR
BUT WE'VE GOT A LOT OF GROUND TO COVER BEFORE IT GETS DARK ...
MOTHER COULDN'T FACE THE FUNERAL.
SHE'S NOT WELL ENOUGH TO LEAVE...
... AND SINCE I'M NOT SURE ...
...WHERE SHE'LL BE GOING...
YOU MUSN'T WORRY, ROBERT!
BUT I DON'T HAVE ANY IDEA WHAT'S TO BECOME OF US!
YOUR FATHER'S FRIENDS WILL HELP YOU.
ALL YOU NEED TO DO IS ASK, ASK ANY ONE OF US — OR ALL OF US!

...THE ENTIRE COUNTRY IS AT YOUR DISPOSAL
THANK YOU, SIR!
LUCY WANTED TO COME...
... BUT UNDER THE CIRCUM-STANCES...
I KNOW YOU MUST BE GOING.
"MY DEAR LUCY,
EDWIN'S HOTEL
THINK NO MORE OF HIM, HE IS DEAD TO US NOW AS HE SOON MUST BE...
KNOCK KNOCK!
... TO ALL THE WORLD."
COME IN!
YOU RANG, SIR ...?
PLEASE DELIVER THIS LETTER.

THERE WILL BE ANOTHER HALF DOLLAR IF YOU WAIT FOR THE REPLY.
WHAT IF THE LADY IS OUT?
SHE WON'T BE...
THERE'S A WOMAN OUT IN THE CORRIDOR.
SOME CURIOSITY SEEKER.
SHE SAYS SHE HAS SOMETHING FOR YOU.
LET ME SEE HER...
SHE'S A BARMAID!
FOR GOD'S SAKE, WHAT ABOUT LUCY?
KEEP HER OUT OF THIS!!
AH, WELL, COME ON IN.
FOR GOD'S SAKE, WHY ARE YOU HERE!?
I'M A FRIEND OF YOUR BROTHER'S. MY NAME IS...
DO NOT TELL ME YOUR NAME... DID YOU KNOW THE POLICE ARE LOOKING FOR YOU?
THE POLICE?
SENATOR HALE AND I BOTH GAVE A DETAILED DESCRIPTION OF YOU. IT WILL BE EASIER IF YOU COME FORWARD BEFORE THEY HUNT YOU DOWN. AND TRUST ME, THEY WILL FIND YOU SOONER OR LATER.

WHAT ABOUT JOHNNIE ?
HAVE YOU LOST YOUR REASON?
THERE'S AN ISABELLE IN NEW YORK, JUST A GIRL REALLY, WHO CLAIMS TO BE PREGNANT WITH HIS CHILD. HE GAVE HER AN INSCRIBED RING, SHE THINKS THEY'RE MARRIED!
NATIONAL HOTEL
WANTED
WANTED
BOOTH
THAT MEANS NOTHING TO ME, HAVE YOU HEARD? IS HE STILL ALIVE?
NOT TO ME!
MY BROTHER DIED AT 7:22 LAST SATURDAY MORNING ALONG WITH OUR BELOVED PRESIDENT.
NOW BE GONE OR I'LL CALL THE POLICE MYSELF!
YOU CLAIM NOT TO KNOW THIS MAN...
...EVEN THOUGH HE WAS SEEN COMING AND GOING FROM THIS HOUSE.
SURRAT
BOOTH
HAROLD
$100,000 REWARD!
THE MURDERER
Of our late beloved President, Abraham Lincoln
IS STILL AT LARGE
$50,000 REWARD
$25,000 REWARD
AS I TOLD YOU, MY SON MIGHT BE ABLE TO HELP YOU.

WE'D LIKE TO SPEAK TO YOUR SON.
HE'S NOT HERE AT THE MOMENT.
Mrs SURRAT BOARD HOUS
WHEN DID YOU LAST SEE HIM, Mrs. SURRATT?
COME ON!
?
I CAME TO DIG OUT THE CELLAR ...
CAUGHT THIS FELLER COMIN' AROUND THE BACK.
IS THAT RIGHT?
DO YOU KNOW THIS MAN?
I... MY SON MADE THE ARRANGEMENTS ...
WELL, UNTIL WE LOCATE YOUR SON, Mrs. SURRATT, I'M AFRAID YOU'LL HAVE TO COME WITH US.
LET'S TAKE THEM ALL FOR QUESTIONING!

MAMA, THEY'RE TAKING AWAY ALL BROTHER'S BOOKS!!
THEY'LL BE RETURNED TO YOU, MISS SURRATT.
HAVE YOU EVER SEEN THIS MAN BEFORE?
I'M NOT SURE ...
MAYBE A NIGHT IN JAIL WILL REFRESH YOUR MEMORY...
TAKE EVERYONE TO HEADQUARTERS! WE'LL CLEAN OUT THIS NEST.
A MARYLAND RIVERBANK

WELL, THIS IS AS FAR AS I GO.
WE CAN'T THANK YOU ENOUGH.
I DIDN'T DO ANY OF THIS FOR MONEY!
NO, OF COURSE NOT!
THIS IS SOMETHING I CAN TELL MY CHILDREN ABOUT ONE DAY.
?
"WHO E'ER REPAYS OUR LOVE WITH LOVE AGAIN
LET PEACE BE JOINED TO LENGTH OF DAYS
LET PEACE BE JOINED TO BLESS HIS HAPPY REIGN.
JOHN WILKES BOOTH"
CATO, TAKE THIS LETTER TO THE POLICE STATION...
TO THE OFFICER WHO TOOK EDWIN AND MY FATHER.
BUT DON'T LET HIM SEE YOU.
MAYBE WE SHOULD WAIT UNTIL THE SENATOR GETS BACK.
IT'S BETTER IF HE DOESN'T KNOW.
THEN MAYBE IT'S BETTER IF YOU TAKE THE NOTE YOURSELF
...
!
IF THEY CONNECT THIS TO MY FATHER, THE SCANDAL WOULD KILL HIM. — YOU DO UNDERSTAND? I HAVE TO PROTECT THE SENATOR!
I'LL LEAVE THE ENVELOPE AT THE DESK.

Dearest
CHLOROFORM
POLICE STATION
I'LL SEE YOU LATER, O'HARA!
ALL RIGHT, HARRIS!
...!
PARDON ME, SIR, JUST DROPPING OFF THIS MESSAGE.
WHO'S IT FROM?
DON'T RIGHTLY KNOW; SOME FELLA GAVE ME FOUR BITS TO TAKE IT TO THE DESK...
DON'T SAY WHO IT'S FOR ...
HEY!
HEY! BOY! COME BACK HERE!
?!
ELLA ...

GOT SOME FOOD AT THE NEXT FARM OVER...
...AND CRIBBED THE PAPERS WHILE THE OLD BIDDY WASN'T LOOKING.
ELLA...
HAVE THEY GOT HER TOO?
SHE TRIED TO KILL HERSELF.
A PILE OF ASHES BY HER... NOTHING ELSE?
NOTHING ELSE...
THE LANDLADY FINDING A PICTURE OF WILKES BOOTH. THAT WAS A LUCKY BREAK.
SHE LOVED THE THEATER, SIR.
SHE TRIED TO KILL HERSELF WITH BOOTH'S PHOTOGRAPH UNDER HER PILLOW!
WE DON'T KNOW IF IT WAS SUICIDE!

HARRIS, MORE THAN FIFTY MEN HAVE DIED DURING OUR SEARCH IN THE SWAMPS OF VIRGINIA.
MEN ARE SCOURING RIVERFRONTS FROM HERE TO NEW ORLEANS...
... PATROLING THE CANADIAN BORDER.
OUR NATION IS ON THE BRINK OF CHAOS.
CIVIL WAR COULD BREAK OUT AGAIN IF WE CAN'T FIND THE ASSASSINS ROAMING FREE!
YES SIR!
GET HER TALKING. THE DOCTOR SAYS SHE HASN'T SPOKEN A WORD SINCE SHE CAME TO.
IF YOU'D LET ME SEE HER ALONE...
THAT WON'T BE POSSIBLE. WE KNOW ABOUT YOUR PREVIOUS RELATIONSHIP AND SO YOU MAY SEE HER...
...BUT ONLY IF YOU GET RESULTS. ...OR ELSE THIS CONNECTION MAY PROVE COSTLY. UNDERSTOOD?
UNDERSTOOD, SIR!
THE VIRGINIA COUNTRYSIDE
LET'S STAY THE NIGHT HERE, AND TAKE THE WAGON IN THE MORNING.
KNOCK! KNOCK!

LUCAS?
WHO'S LOOKING FOR HIM?
STUART SAID YOU'VE GOT A WAGON FOR HIRE.
MY BROTHER AND ME NEED A RIDE INTO PORT CONWAY...
IT'S LATE.
WE'LL GO IN THE MORNING.
I CAN'T BE TAKING IN WHITE PEOPLE.
WE'RE CONFEDERATE SOLDIERS ...
IN SERVICE THREE YEARS AND IN NEED OF A PLACE TO STAY!
MY WIFE IS SICK AND WE ONLY HAVE ONE ROOM!
WE INTEND TO STAY!
I THOUGHT YOU'D BE DONE PRESSING IN THE NORTHERN NECK SINCE THE...?!
...FALL OF RICHMOND ...
SAY THAT AGAIN!
...
THAT'S RIGHT, OLD MAN!

WE'LL SPEND THE NIGHT HERE, TAKE THE WAGON IN THE MORNING.
THE PORT CONWAY FERRY, APRIL 24
WHAT DO WE OWE YOU?
I USUALLY GET TEN IN GOLD OR TWENTY IN GREENBACKS ...
THANK YOU!
WHERE ARE YOU BOYS HEADED ?
CROSSING THE RAPPAHANNOCK. WHERE ARE YOU HEADED?

Chapter 8

Wherein:

- A revived Ella sets the Army on Booth's trail, at the urging of her soldier beau.
- Booth and Davy, resting briefly at a farm in Virginia, arouse the suspicions of their hosts.
- On April 26, 1865, John Wilkes Booth arrives at his inevitable, ignominious end.

ELLA ...
I KNOW WHAT WILL HAPPEN IF I DON'T HELP YOU...
SO I WANTED YOU TO KNOW THAT JOHN-NIE TOLD ME IF I EVER GOT HURT...
... I COULD FIND Dr. SAMUEL MUDD, HE HAS A PLACE OUT NEAR BRYANTOWN.
WOULD YOU KNOW HIM IF YOU SAW HIM ?
JOHNNIE MET WITH HIM AT THE NATIONAL HOTEL BEFORE CHRISTMAS.
HE TOLD ME TO REMEMBER HIS NAME BECAUSE HE WORKED FOR THE REBEL UNDERGROUND ...
AS SOON AS I CAN MARRY MY SWEET-HEART IN BOWLING GREEN,
I'LL BE HEADING SOUTH AGAIN.
WHY'S THAT?
GOING TO RAISE A COMMAND...

...HITCHING UP WITH MOSBY'S RANGERS... THEN WE'LL HEAD FOR MEXICO.
EXACTLY! IT'S TIME TO ORGANIZE A COUNTERSTRIKE! NOW WITH THE YANKEES RUN-NING SCARED ...
ARE YOU HEADED HOME?
WE'VE BEEN ROBBED OF OUR HOMELAND!
DO I KNOW YOU?
PATRIOTS, SIR, MERE PATRIOTS ...
...SEEKING TO REDEEM THE HONOR OF OUR LOST CAUSE
ARE YOU WHO I THINK YOU ARE?
THE ASSASSINATORS!!
I THOUGHT SO... BY GOD, I'VE CROSSED THE RIVER WITH JOHN WILKES BOOTH!
LET'S HOPE WE'VE REACHED THE PROMISED LAND.

IT'S GRATIFYING TO MEET SOMEONE WHO CAN BE SO VALUABLE IN THE NEW REGIME...
A REAL HONOR!
...BUT YOU COULD BE OF EVEN GREATER SERVICE.
WE NEED A PLACE TO STAY FOR A SHORT TIME, SO MY LEG CAN HEAL.
THE DOCTOR'S BEEN IDENTIFIED AS MEMBER OF THE REBEL UNDERGROUND!
BUT MUDD WAS ALREADY INTERROGATED!
DID THEY SEARCH HIS HOME?
!...
YOU'RE SO FIRED UP ABOUT THIS YOU CAN GO YOURSELF!
FIND A LIEUTENANT LOVETT AND REPORT BACK!
THANK YOU, SIR!
IF THIS TURNS INTO SOMETHING, YOU'LL BE GETTING THOSE SERGEANT'S STRIPES.
YES, SIR!

SAMUEL MUDD'S FARM
I TOLD YOU, Lt. LOVETT, I NEVER SAW THE MAN BEFORE.
ARE YOU IN THE HABIT OF OPENING UP YOUR HOME TO STRANGERS, IN THE MIDDLE OF THE NIGHT?
WELL, Mr. TYSON - THAT WAS HIS NAME - WAS IN SUCH A LOT OF PAIN...
... AND HIS BROTHER BEGGED US FOR HELP, AND OFFERED US GOLD.
SO THE MONEY INTERESTED YOU?
IT'S NOT THE WAY YOU'RE MAKING IT SOUND!
THESE STRANGERS LEFT ON SATURDAY AND YOU HAVEN'T SEEN OR HEARD FROM THEM SINCE?
NO, NOT AT ALL!
AND THEY DIDN'T LEAVE ANYTHING BEHIND?
THAT BOOT, SAMUEL ...
... THE ONE I FOUND UNDER THE BED.
WHAT BOOT? CAN YOU GET IT FOR ME?
Dr. MUDD ...

...YOU HAD SEEN AT LEAST ONE OF THEM BEFORE.
I DON'T UNDER-STAND!
You'D MET JOHN WILKES BOOTH IN SURRATTVILLE LAST FALL?
YES, THAT'S RIGHT.
SO WHEN YOU TOLD HARDY LAST WEEK YOU DIDN'T KNOW BOOTH, YOU WERE NOT EXACTLY BEING TRUTHFUL...
I'D MET HIM, BUT I WASN'T SURE WHICH OF THE BROTHERS IT WAS, SO I THOUGHT NO, I DON'T KNOW HIM.
I SEE...
WHICH BROTHER DID YOU MEET IN THE NATIONAL HOTEL LAST DECEMBER, Dr. MUDD?
JOE, LOOK AT THIS!!!
H.LUX
Maker • 445 BROADWAY
J. Wilkes
Dr. MUDD, YOU'LL HAVE TO COME WITH US!

BUT I COOPERATED! I CAN'T LEAVE MY WIFE AND CHILDREN!
YOU SHOULD HAVE THOUGHT OF THAT BEFORE HARBORING A MURDERER...
WHAT!?
WE'LL GO STRAIGHT TO WASHINGTON... YOU'LL MAKE ARRANGEMENTS WHILE I SEND A TELEGRAM.
WAR DEPARTMENT, LATER THAT DAY
WE HAVE THIS BOOT AND HE WAS SEEN WITH ANOTHER MAN HEADING INTO ZEKIAH SWAMP.
THAT WAS OVER A WEEK AGO!
HE COULD BE ANYWHERE BY NOW!!
HE WAS SIGHTED ON CRUTCHES AND CAN'T HAVE GOTTEN FAR...
275
302
WE'LL CONCENTRATE OUR EFFORTS IN VIRGINIA AND SMOKE HIM OUT, Mr. SECRETARY...
THIS COUNTRY IS TEETERING ON THE BRINK, CAPTAIN. OUR NATION HAS LOST ITS GREATEST LEADER...
...AND I HAVE LOST AN IRREPLACE-ABLE FRIEND.

I UNDERSTAND, Mr. SECRETARY...
THE ONLY CURE IS TO BRING THOSE RESPONSIBLE TO JUDGMENT.
ONLY THROUGH VENGEANCE WILL OUR NATION BE SAVED.
PORT ROYAL FERRY
YOU'LL BE WILLING TO TALK TO US, TO HELP US?
FOLKS 'ROUND HERE NOT TOO BROKEN UP ABOUT THE PRESIDENT'S PASSING...
...BUT MY WIFE CRIED HER EYES OUT WHEN THE PRESIDENT DIED!
I GOT MY COUSIN TO RUN THE FERRY AND TOOK HER UP TO WASHINGTON TO SEE HIS FUNERAL TRAIN.
WE CAN KEEP ANY INFORMATION CONFIDENTIAL, BUT CAN YOU TELL ME, HAVE YOU EVER SEEN THESE MEN?
...
...SEEN THESE TWO!
YOU'RE SURE?!
WHEN DID YOU LAST SEE THEM?

MUST HAVE BEEN ...
... A COUPLE OF DAYS AGO.
WHICH WAY WERE THEY HEADED?
DON'T RIGHTLY KNOW ...
... BUT THEY WAS TALKING WITH A SOLDIER NAMED JETT...
... HEADED TO SEE HIS GIRL IN BOWLING GREEN.
WOULDN'T HAPPEN TO KNOW THE GIRL'S NAME, WOULD YOU?
HER DADDY OWNS THE STAR HOTEL.
ALL RIGHT. MEN, A HARD RIDE TO BOWLING GREEN!!
LOCUST HILL, GARRETT'S FARM APRIL 25, 1865
YOU MAKE IT ALL SOUND SO EXCITING, Mr. BOYD!
IT'S ONLY EXCITING IF YOU LIVE TO TELL THE TALE, MISS GARRETT.
YOUR BROTHER HEADED OFF TO TOWN TO GET THE PAPERS.
DAVY'S GOT A KEEN INTEREST IN CURRENT EVENTS.

PAPA SAYS IT'S NOT SAFE TO TAKE IN STRANGERS SINCE THE WAR ENDED...
... YOU NEVER KNOW.
WE'RE SO PLEASED WILLIAM JETT SENT YOU AND YOUR BROTHER OUR WAY, Mr. BOYD! DON'T PAY ANY ATTENTION TO OUR SISTER.
SHE'S RIGHT. YOU CAN'T BE TOO CAREFUL.
?
I HEAR HORSES IN THE DISTANCE ...
!
NEW YORK REGIMENT!
Mr. BOYD, Mr. BOYD!
IS THERE SOMETHING WRONG?

LUCY HALE'S HOME
YOU'RE THE ONLY ONE I CAN TALK TO ABOUT THIS ...

SO HE THOUGHT IT WAS HIS FATE TO DO THIS TERRIBLE DEED AND BE PUNISHED.

MY BROTHER COULD NOT HAVE BEEN THINKING AT ALL.

OUR MOTHER PRAYS THAT HE WON'T SURVIVE CAPTURE BECAUSE SHE CANNOT STAND WATCHING HIM HANG.

THE SENATOR'S CARRIAGE IS COMING.
I MUST CATCH THE TRAIN TO NEW YORK, LUCY!

... AND THEY CAME BACK TO THE HOUSE AS SOON AS THE SOLDIERS GOT PAST.

IF WILLIAM JETT VOUCHES FOR 'EM ...
SOMETHING JUST ISN'T RIGHT! ...
PUT 'EM IN THE BARN, SON!
LET'S LOCK 'EM IN!
WE'LL SLEEP OUT IN THE CRIB, MAKE SURE THEY STAY PUT.
I'LL SEND OVER TO BOWLING GREEN IN THE MORNING.
THUMP!
?!
LAY DOWN YOUR ARMS !!!
THE STAR HOTEL, BOWLING GREEN
WE'VE GOT THE PLACE SURROUNDED!
UH?

WHAT'S GOING ON ?!
GET THAT WOMAN OUT OF HERE!
!
WHERE ARE YOU TAKING HER?
THAT DEPENDS ON YOU, JETT.
WE HAVE EYEWITNESSES THAT YOU LEFT THE PORT ROYAL FERRY WITH TWO MEN.
SHE'LL BE RELEASED ONCE WE FIND THE SUSPECTS.
I... I SENT THEM TO A FARM NEAR THE ROAD TO PORT ROYAL ...
ROUND UP EVERY ABLE-BODIED MAN YOU CAN FIND!
WE'LL HEAD OUT IN A QUARTER HOUR.
YES, SIR!
INSIDE GARRETT'S BARN
THEY LOCKED US IN?...

DON'T PANIC, DAVY.
I WANT TO GO HOME, WILKES.
I CAN'T TAKE THIS!
I KNOW IT IS HARD...
BUT IF WE CAN JUST HANG ON UNTIL THE UPRISING ...
IT'S BEEN MORE THAN A WEEK...
LOOKS LIKE PEOPLE ARE TIRED OF FIGHTING.
OF COURSE THEY ARE, BUT ONCE THEY FIND OUT THERE ARE TRUE WARRIORS WILLING TO STRIKE...
...WE'LL HUNT DOWN THE DOGS AND COWARDS.
WE'RE THE ONES LIVING LIKE DOGS.

WHAT ARE YOU WRITING ?
OUR HISTORY, DAVY.
A CHRONICLE OF THE INGLORIOUS BUT THRILLING TALE OF HOW WE TRIED TO SAVE THE CONFEDERACY FROM ITSELF.
"TONIGHT, I ESCAPE THE BLOOD HOUNDS ONCE MORE. WHO, WHO CAN READ HIS FATE? GOD'S WILL BE DONE."
"I HAVE TOO GREAT A SOUL TO DIE LIKE A CRIMINAL."
"O, MAY HE, MAY HE SPARE ME THAT AND LET ME DIE BRAVELY!"

ALL SECURE, BOYS?
WHAT'S ALL THE RUCKUS ?!
TAKE IT EASY, FARMER GARRETT!
YOU'VE GOT SOMETHING WE WANT...
LET MY SONS GO!
...AND WE'VE GOT SOMETHING YOU WANT.
ABOUT THOSE TWO STRANGERS ...
...WHO CAME THROUGH HERE EARLY THIS MORNING... ONE ON CRUTCHES.
WHAT HAVE THEY DONE?
CAUSED YOU A LOT OF TROUBLE.
TOSS A ROPE OVER ONE OF THOSE LOCUST TREES!
YES, SIR!

PICK WHICH ONE YOU WANT US TO START WITH, Mr. GARRETT
IT'S YOUR CHOICE.
...
THEY'RE IN THE BARN.
?!
SOLDIERS WANT YOU TO COME ON OUT ...
YOU HAVEN'T IMPLICATED ME!?
WHA... WHAT IS IT, WILKES?
AM I TO BE BETRAYED BY FRIENDS ?

I'LL...
I'LL GO OUT FIRST, WILKES.
NO!
YOU CAN'T ESCAPE. GIVE YOURSELF UP!
YOU HAVE TEN MINUTES!
IF YOU DON'T THROW OUT YOUR WEAPONS WE'LL BURN THE BARN DOWN!

THE ONE WITH THE BAD LEG IS ARMED TO THE TEETH ...
THE OTHER ONE WANTS TO SURRENDER.
GIVE UP YOUR ARMS OR THE BUILDING WILL BE SET AFIRE!
GIVE THEM MORE TIME...
I'M COMING OUT!
DAVY, WHAT ARE YOU DOING ?!
COME BACK HERE!!!

YOU HAVE FIVE MINUTES!
I'M NOTHING BUT A CRIPPLE. I'VE BUT ONE LEG,
YOU OUGHT TO GIVE ME A CHANCE FOR
A FAIR FIGHT

THIS IS NO CHILD'S PLAY!
WE ARE IN EARNEST AND WILL CARRY OUT OUR THREATS...
FIVE MINUTES

START THE FIRE!
PAW!

GET HIM OUT!
CAN WE MOVE HIM YET, DOC?
I THOUGHT WE MIGHT SAVE HIM ...

... BUT HE'S LOST TOO MUCH BLOOD FROM THE WOUND IN HIS NECK.
PUT HIM ON THE MATTRESS ...

KILL ME ...
SHH, TAKE SOMETHING TO DRINK!
IT MAY TAKE A LONG TIME ... BUT HE CAN'T SURVIVE.
SIR ?
I DIDN'T TELL ANYONE TO FIRE, PRIVATE CORBETT!
HE STARTED COMING OUT WITH HIS GUN RAISED...
THE GENERAL ORDER WAS TO TAKE SUSPECTS ALIVE!
IT'S NEARLY OVER
HE'S TRYING TO SPEAK.
... TELL MY MOTHER THAT I DID IT FOR MY COUNTRY...
... THAT I DIE FOR MY COUNTRY! ...
... USELESS ...
USELESS.
GIDDY UP
DY UP HORSEY,
DON'T SAY STOP
JUST LET YOUR FEET GO
CLIPPETY CLOP
CLIPPETY CLOP AND HIPPITY HOP,
WE'RE HOMEWARD BOUND

Chapter 9

Wherein:

- Our story draws to a close.
- Booth's fellow conspirators join him in an anonymous grave, unmarked but not entirely unmourned.
- Bit by bit, Lucy Hale begins to reclaim a life torn apart by war and men's passions.

UNION SHIP "MONTAUK," SEVERAL DAYS LATER
HALT!
PERMISSION TO BOARD, SIR...
WELCOME ONBOARD, SIR!
YOU'RE TAKING EXTRAORDINARY PRECAUTIONS, Sgt. HARRIS!
NO ONE GETS ON-BOARD, SIR, WITHOUT AN EYEBALL INSPECTION!
GOOD WORK!
YOU MUST HAVE A HARD TIME KEEPING THE PRESS AT BAY...
ONLY A COUPLE HAVE GONE INTO THE DRINK.

WE'LL DO WHAT WE HAVE TO DO, SIR.
SOME
WE DIDN'T REALLY CATCH HIM, THAT IT'S ALL A HOAX.
WE'VE HAD TWO DOCTORS INSPECT THE BODY. THERE CAN'T BE NO DOUBT
WE CAUGHT HIM AND WE INTEND TO KEEP HIM.
NO HONOR GUARD AND FUNERAL TRAIN FOR THIS TRAITOR!
YES INDEED Sgt. HARRIS, CARRY ON!
ALONG THE POTOMAC
A "BURIAL AT SEA"...
OBSERVED...
...BY ONE WHO IS HIMSELF OBSERVED, AND FINALLY APPREHENDED.

WASHINGTON ARSENAL
AND YOU'RE SURE YOU CAN MANAGE TO KEEP THIS BETWEEN US, PRIVATE?
YOU KEPT YOUR MOUTH SHUT WHEN YOU FOUND ME SLEEPING ON PICKET DUTY ...
NO SENSE LOSING GOOD MEN TO THE HANGMAN'S NOOSE.
AND YOU HAVE PROVEN A FINE SOLDIER.
THIS IS SOMETHING TO BE BURIED ...
... DEAD AND BURIED.
I'LL TAKE CARE OF IT!
KEEP OUT

JUDGMENT DAY
JULY 7, 1865
LEWIS PAYNE
DAVY HEROLD
GEORGE ADZERODT
MEMENTO
Born, February 12
Assassinated, April 1
MARY SURRATT

WATCH THE STEP, Mrs. SURRATT!

THE HALE HOME
YOU WANT EVERYTHING SENT TO NEW HAMPSHIRE,
DON'T WANT TO HOLD ANY TRUNKS HERE IN WASHINGTON, MISS LUCY.
I'LL MAKE SURE THE DRAY DRIVER CAN GET THESE TRUNKS TO THE STATION IN TIME.
THANK YOU, CATO ...
YOU'LL MAKE A FRESH START WHEN WE GET TO MADRID.
FAR FROM WAGGING TONGUES AND DANGLING NOOSES,...
DON'T LET SUCH THOUGHTS PREY ON YOU, LUCY!
THE SECRETARY OF WAR ASSURED ME YOUR NAME WOULD NEVER COME UP.
YOU MEAN THAT YOUR NAME WOULD NEVER COME UP!
IS THAT WHAT YOU THINK?
THAT I WORRY OVER MY CAREER?
OH, PAPA, I'M SO WRONG ABOUT EVERYTHING!!

...AND I WANTED TO THANK YOU PERSONALLY ...
WAR DEPARTMENT, JULY 8, 1865
... FOR YOUR ROLE IN BRINGING THE CONSPIRATORS TO JUSTICE.
THE TRIAL COULDN'T HAVE GONE BETTER.
I DIDN'T KNOW CIVILIANS COULD BE TRIED IN A MILITARY COURT.
WE HAD TO DO WHAT WAS IN THE BEST INTERESTS OF OUR COUNTRY,
SWIFT AND SURE JUSTICE, ADMINISTERED WITHOUT DELAY...
YES, SIR, BUT WHEN WE RETURN THE DECEASED TO THEIR FAMILIES...
AS LONG AS I HAVE BREATH IN MY BODY...

THAT BASTARD BOOTH'S BODY WILL REMAIN IN GOVERNMENT CUSTODY...
...
YES, SIR ...
...AND IN HELL.
UNDERSTOOD, SIR. BUT THE OTHERS?
THEY CAN ROT WITH HIM!
I WILL NOT LET ANY OF THEM STEAL A SINGLE DROP OF MARTYR-DOM FROM OUR BELOVED PRESIDENT.
OF COURSE, SIR!
NOT EVEN THAT WOMAN MRS. SURRATT!
NONE OF THEM WILL BE ALLOWED A PROPER BURIAL?
YOU HEARD ME, CAPTAIN. DISMISSED!
C.C. COLBERT & TANITOC 20-6-09

Epilogue

Three years later the Booth clan reconvened in Green Mount Cemetary in Baltimore. Lacking a proper grave site, John Wilkes Booth was remembered by his relations at the site of their family vault.

Lucy Hale was one of their party. The gathering provided an opportunity for Lucy and Edwin to make their peace, and for Lucy to say her goodbyes to John Wilkes Booth.

Author's Note

When I was just a child, I loved history and spent a lot of time visiting historic sites with my parents. I do remember getting worn out by their insistence that we attend all the local Civil War centennial festivities in the 1960s. However, more than forty years later, I treasure the memory of these events. Pageantry, mystery, and intense patriotism seemed to surround certain aspects of the past.

When I decided to pursue a career teaching and writing American history, I had no idea how important these childhood memories might become, connecting me to the core of my passion for the past. Two Ivy League degrees later and my first dozen books on the shelf, and it became more and more challenging to conjure up the youthful enthusiasm that lured me back into nineteenth century America. It can be hard to reconcile the imaginative distortions of childhood memory with the rigorous scholarship an academic consumes and creates.

However, I remain intrigued by living historians, by reenactors, by heritage interpreters—by people and places that encourage different drummers and create complex interpretations of the past's importance in our everyday lives. History becomes something immediate and relatable in these contexts, as it often does in art: film, literature, and purely visual media. Graphic novels—long-form narrative comics—combine the latter two elements into a form that lends itself surprisingly well to historical fiction. The idea that comic books can only offer a simplistic vision clearly ignores dramatic evidence otherwise. A growing body of historical graphic novels such as Guibert's *Alan's War* boast strong characters, vivid images, and powerful narrative arcs that clearly complicate and improve a story.

By the turn of the twenty-first century, my own two teenaged sons had become enthralled by the rising tide of graphic novels—from manga flooding out from Japan to *bande dessinée* (literally "drawn strip") spiralling outward from France. As a writer, I became fascinated by the primal appeal of the form and became aware of their near-narcotic qualities. And so, instead of watching this literature from the sidelines, I decided to enter the fray.

As the author of nearly two dozen books in American history, I have periodically consigned myself to long periods of exile in libraries and archives. I have been lucky enough to have generous, sharing colleagues, and several co-editors over the years. But the scholar's life can be isolated and frustrating. I have sometimes become despondent over the lack of scholarly resources available to bring my historical figures to life.

So when I took on writing the script for *Booth*, I understood that here, in addition to bringing the rigorous tools of my craft into play, I could now indulge in the musings and speculations often denied to scholars.

I was thrilled to be delving into the world of fiction. As a committed historian, I could not abandon authenticity with *Booth*—but struggled to imagine what "might have been," alongside what very likely was. Good historical fiction attempts to integrate both. History is always full of doubt and debate, as well as the rich unfolding of secrets the past has locked away.

I felt very lucky that when I started writing my manuscript, I could draw on several new and exciting studies of Booth and the assassination—books such as James Swanson and Daniel Weinberg's *Lincoln's Assassins: Their Trial and Execution* [2001], Elizabeth Leonard's *Lincoln's Avengers: Justice, Revenge, and Reunion after the Civil War* [2004], and most especially Michael W. Kauffman's *American Brutus: John Wilkes Booth and the Lincoln Conspiracies* [2004]. I was fortunate to have terrific recent resources such as Timothy S. Good's *We Saw Lincoln Shot: One Hundred Eyewitness Accounts* [1996], John Rhodehamel and Louise Taper's *Right or Wrong, God Judge Me: The Writings Of John Wilkes Booth* [1997], and Terry Alford's *John Wilkes Booth: A Sister's Memoir by Asia Booth Clarke* [1999]. I appreciated both James L. Swanson's *Manhunt: The 12-Day Chase for Lincoln's Killer* [2006] and Sarah Vowell's inspirational *Assassination Vacation* [2005].

I was unable to make use of several new fine studies, including Kate Clifford Larson's 2008 study of Mary Surratt, *The Assassin's Accomplice: Mary Surratt and the Plot to Kill Abraham Lincoln* and Edward Steers and Harold Holzer's *The Lincoln Assassination Conspirators: Their Confinement and Execution, As Recorded in the Letterbook of John Frederick Hartranft* [2009]. New ideas will continue and the parade of fascinating, imaginative material, I trust, will never end.

Booth reimagines those chaotic days when we regained a nation but lost Abraham Lincoln. It underscores the multiple consequences created by a desperately dramatic twenty-six-year-old who changed the course of American history. I hope this book will be only a beginning for those interested in our first presidential assassination, and especially those keen to know more about our sixteenth president.

This project is part of my desire to move toward a changing future. From Dante's *Inferno*: "midway in the journey...I came to myself in a dark wood, for the straight way was lost." Constructing an innovative narrative of time and place; slaking a thirst for history that can cohabit with imagined worlds, these and other adventures await those writers and readers willing to lose ourselves in the dark wood. And because I can confess to being "Forlorn No More," this book represents a wonderful opportunity to find companions on the journey. Along the way, Tanitoc, my fantastical collaborator, has brought to life characters who are both mine and yours, as well as history's, and constructed a world of images to enrich and complicate my world of words. I am thrilled to launch this book, my twenty-fifth, out into the world, but wish to thank Calista Brill, Mark Siegel, and the whole First Second family. I would be remiss not to thank my two sons, Ned and Drew Colbert, and their father Daniel, who gave me the special encouragement I needed to complete this book.

-C. C. Colbert